AF433317

*Filippo Pasqui*

# L'ONDHON

Translated by Chiara Mapelli

# Recurring Symbols

Within this book, you will find multiple points of view, narrated by different people. Below, you can find the symbols to recognise who is speaking. In order of appearance:

-   \-   Gaetano
-   \-   **Marco Valdo, the interviewer**
-   ∨   Yu, Gaetano's flatmate
-   +   Alessandro, Gaetano's flatmate
-   <   Lorenzo
-   ~   Serena
-   =   Gaetano's customer
-   •   Enrico, the restaurant's barman
-   ¤   Sandro, the restaurant's host
-   □   Fabio, the stranger at the fair
-   ∴   Soho's shop assistant
-   ♠   The presenter of DOGE event
-   ♣   Paolo, working at DOGE event
-   ♦   Roberta, working at DOGE event
-   √   The guy collecting signatures
-   ∧   Charlotte, Serena's host
-   #   Aasha, Lorenzo's business partner

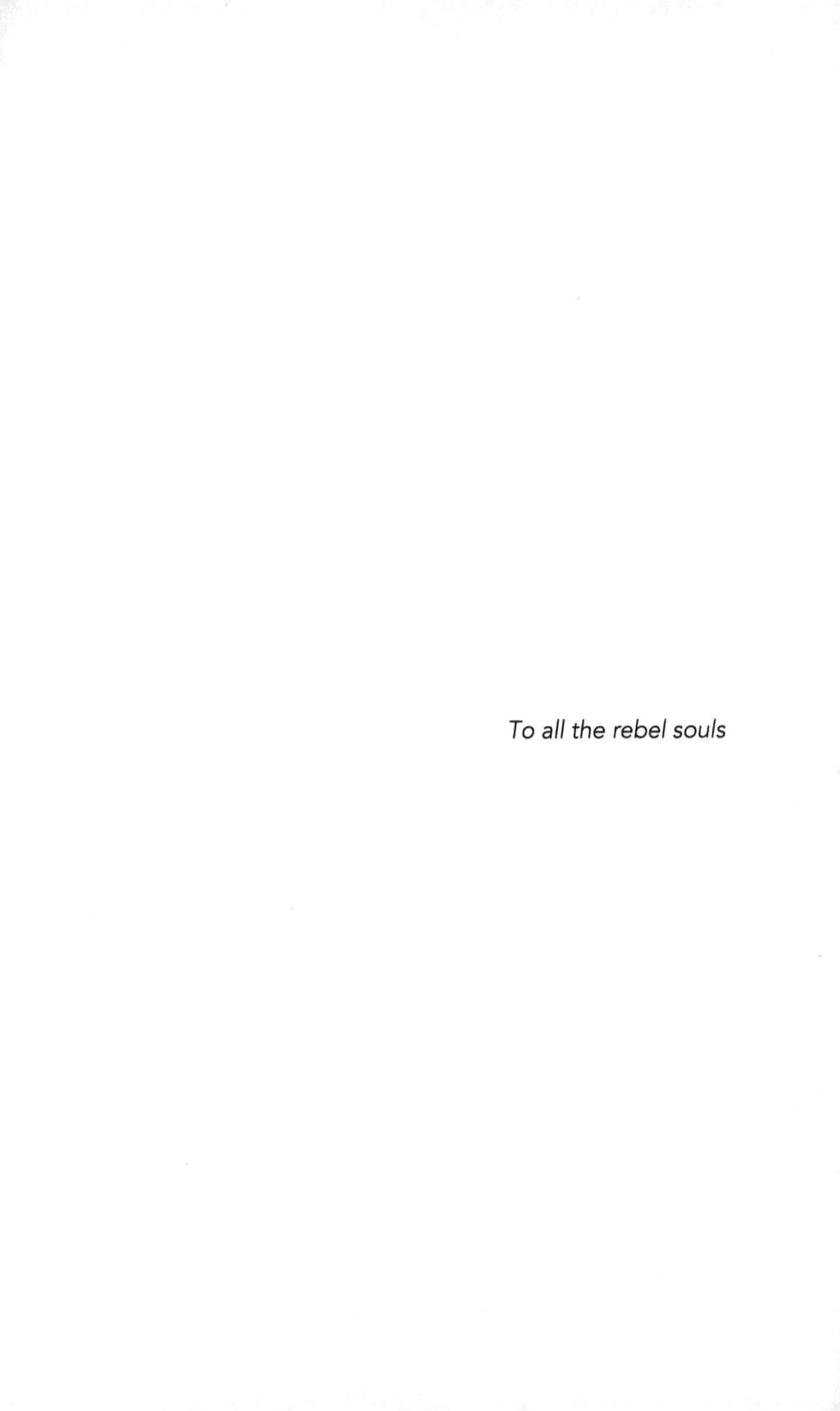

*To all the rebel souls*

Studies show that young Italians feel like outcasts.

Some of them, mindful of this issue, decide to move abroad
to improve their lives.

This is known as the so-called "brain drain", even when
whoever is moving abroad does not have a degree.

To understand this event, the author Marco Valdo
spent some time in London, living with some of those who
decided to move.

Below are the interviews that took place over that period.

1

- Here, here. Welcome! How was your journey? Welcome to Wood Green! Nice to meet you, I'm Gaetano. You're quite lucky you know, today is my day off. We are always so busy over at the restaurant, and when I have a day off, I get to fully recharge.
Come in, let me show you around.
This is the kitchen, the only common area of the house. Apart from the bathroom, of course. There are six of us living here, and the flat has only one bathroom and a kitchen. It's not much but we're okay with it.
Ah, she is Yu, I think she's like Chinese, or something like that, I mean.
Hey Yu, he is my friend from Italy!
What is your name again?
- **Marco.**
- He is Marco, from Italy!
v Hi Marco. *[Yu leaves the kitchen].*
- Yeah okay, fuck off.
Please close the door, Marco.
I honestly can't stand her. She never talks to anyone in this house. I don't even know what she does. When I'm in here, she is always locked in her room and the few times we meet in the kitchen she is always making those weird spaghetti-like things they eat in Asia, or she is steaming some meat, without any oil, just like that. Horrible stuff, yuck.

Apart from the fact that oil sucks here, so maybe I do agree with her to some extent. Ah, what can you do?

So, would you like anything? An English breakfast, some coffee? Unfortunately, I only have instant coffee as I forgot to bring the proper coffee machine over here, damn.

Anyway, look, when I first moved, I used to say, "Watery coffee is disgusting, the only good coffee is the one we make at home in Italy", but after a while - needs must - I tried this one [*he shows us a coffee bag by a famous American company which makes instant coffee*] and let me tell you, it's actually okay to drink. You just need to add a little bit of milk and there you go; it's almost like an espresso macchiato.

My father would most certainly not agree. Back where I'm from, when you drink your coffee, you need to have a tiny glass of sparkling water on the side. You need to drink your water before the coffee, to rinse your mouth for it.

What do you even know though, you're from the North of Italy! "*Cotoleeetta, cadrega, pirla*[1]", [*he laughs*].

- **To be fair, I am from Tuscany.**

Well, always a Northern, though, come on now! Take this coffee now, *taaaac!*

In Ciociaria, I rarely see people from the North. Perhaps just some businessmen with a big car coming down every week or so, just to have a look at one of their company's branches, or some salesmen with some beat-up car trying to make ends meet by selling stuff on impromptu shops. Even in summer you rarely get to see tourists.

Well yes, near my village, called Ceprano - in the province of Frosinone - we have some small places people like to visit, if only to shoot a few Instagram's stories, but not much more. Most of the times those who end up in Ceprano are lost tourists trying to get to some other place.

---

[1] These are some of the most common words used in the dialect of the region of Lombardy.

Yeah, I guess the only people who come into my village are truck drivers. Maybe those, yes. We have a couple of spots where they stop to grab a bite. They are rather strategic places, as the A1 motorway is just around the corner. Rather than eating quickly at a service station, they stop and eat a more substantial meal and maybe they even pay the same price for it. They're definitely not idiots.

I was born and raised in this magical world.

Wait for a second, I just need to nip to the loo before I start telling you my story. Do you need to go as well? If you want, Alessandro is next door. He is the only Italian guy who - apart from myself - lives in this house. He does make me feel much less lonely. I think he too must be off today, go have a chat with him!


2


*[I knock on Gaetano's flatmate and after a few seconds, a rather sleepy and burly guy opens the door].*
**- Hey, nice to meet you. Do you fancy telling me something about Gaetano?**
+ No.
*[He shuts the door in my face].*


3


- Here we are, where were we? Ah yes, Ceprano. Well, what can I say? I spent twenty years of my life over there, there is not much to say.
**- Why would you not want to talk about it?**
- Well, because I'm a romantic like that. Living here makes me feel nostalgic about older times, but then I think about it and I'm aware that this is not something to hold onto. You know, my days had very little meaning. I spent every day sleeping *[he*

*rolls a joint whilst talking]* and playing videogames. My parents would always yell at me because they could not stand to see me like that, they would tell me "Go help your uncle chop some wood", "There is a window company which has just opened up behind Luciano's house, go ask if they are looking for labourers". And I would always say "Yes, I will go have a look tomorrow", and then I would never do it. And you know why? Because I would tell myself: "Why do it? I'm comfortable how I am now". As in, I was okay with that life in the end.

To be fair, it was not always like that: I used to be a rather ambitious young guy… Fancy a hit?

**- No, no, thank you.**

**Why, how old are you now?**

- Twenty-one.

When I say "young", I mean the years after secondary school. I had quite a few interesting experiences, I feel as if I had to speedily grow up.

You know, those were the times when vaping was about to be a trend.

Do you know which ones I am talking about? Yeah those. I was one of the first people to be obsessed with it because this guy who was my cousin's friend, Emanuele, made me vape for the first time before it was even a thing in Ceprano.

I got to know this guy, Emanuele, thanks to my cousin, yes. I had never seen him before: he must have been around twenty-eight or twenty-nine years old. From Caserta.

Anyhow, we met up at the beach around a month earlier, around Formia, and in those days this Emanuele guy went to visit my cousin. We were playing Call of Duty while chatting about those thingies I had never seen before.

The conversation got so intense that my cousin was not even able to join in, the poor fool. After a while, Emanuele told me "Where I come from, vaping shops are popping up like crazy, *guagliò[2]*", so I told him "This stuff is powerful, *compà[3]*, I believe you". And he told me "You know what, it would be cool to do something like this here!" and I told him that yes, that was a fantastic idea indeed.

You know how nineteen-year-olds are, don't you? Full of enthusiasm and drive, willingness to take on the world? Well, the same thing happened to me.

A few days later, he got in touch and he told me that he was serious about that business we discussed, he wanted to open a shop in Ceprano, and he wanted me as his partner. I said yes immediately, without having a single second thought. Mainly because up until then I had only had a few small jobs, nothing serious, and I was looking forward to something which could have been the opportunity of a lifetime.

Hold on a second, I need to open the window as my flatmates don't have to know that I have been smoking in the kitchen, they would kill me. One of them, some Polish girl - what a bitch - keeps bothering me: I can't smoke in the kitchen, I can't run up the stairs, I can't use other people's pans, I can't even have music in my bedroom. I can't do anything in this house. Sometimes I think about how lucky I was in in my old place: some house share close to Walthamstow with fourteen Italian people, where everybody could do anything they wanted.

Anyway, what was I saying?

**- Something about starting this new venture with Emanuele.**

Ah yes, anyway I accepted his offer and we split our duties: he said he would take care of the administrative side of it, while I was in charge of finding a place for us to rent. You know, these are post-crisis times, there were a plenty of unoccupied shops in Ceprano, and there still are, even in rather decent areas. I found one right next to the local Conad[4] and I used some of my

---

[2] Expression similar to "mate", used in the region of Campania, South Italy.
[3] Expression similar to "mate", used in Ciociaria region and Sicily.
[4] One of the most famous chains of supermarkets, like Tesco.

grandma's money - God rest her soul - to rent it for the first month, plus a sum for the deposit. I gave the contract to Emanuele as I really don't understand anything about any of that stuff. A month later, Emanuele had forged relations with the suppliers. In short, we opened up a nice little shop. I kind of lost sight of my cousin at that time, and the same thing happened with Emanuele, but this helped us strengthen our own relationship.

A little before the opening, we gave ourselves other duties: I would have to remain in the shop to sell the merchandise - vapes, the various flavours and gadgets, which I had tried a couple of days before, and coming up with stories about them which would have appealed to customers - while Emanuele would oversee the more managerial side of the business, such as suppliers' relations and those things, visiting the shop once a month.

All of my friends came to the opening, as well as my relatives and many other people I have known all my life. Emanuele could not come as he was not feeling well, but I made pace with it eventually.

That day was one of the most intense of my whole life.

For five days in a row, virtually the whole town came, and I sold the majority of the vapes I had, even if I had to ask my grandma for some more money to buy more products. She was happy to lend me the money, as I was sure that Emanuele would give it all back to me at the end of the second month with all the accrued interest it would come with it.

We were one of the first ones in Ceprano to open a vaping store, and it quickly became a trend among people of my age. I stayed in the shop all day, I put whatever money we earned on the side, and at the end of the week Emanuele would come and we would split it: I got six hundred euros and he would get the rest of the money. In the first month I bought myself a new PlayStation 4 as well as GTA V. I should have given that money to my grandma, but I told her that unfortunately I had not made enough and that I could not give her any [*he winks at me*].

The second month was a hit as well, people would even come from outside the town to buy from us, even though toward the end of the month, everybody disappeared. Like that, in the blink of an eye. Maybe it was because every smoker in Ceprano now had a vape pen, or maybe because in the neighbouring town, Arce, a new vaping shop had just opened, selling slightly cheaper products. I don't even know, I never fully understood what happened there.

My grandma covered the second month's rent, she was so sweet. However, she told me that that would have been the last time, rightly so. My parents were pressuring me into asking Emanuele to give me all the money that I had put into the company back, though I did not think that Emanuele was to blame. He was a good-looking chap, who kept his promises.

And then yeah, something awful happened at the very end of the month. The worst day of my life, I remember that day as if it were yesterday: overnight, they broke into the shop and stole everything. I lost everything, all the vape pens, the flavours, the gadgets, the earnings from that week and even the receipts. You can't imagine how much I cried when the ladies from Conad called me the morning after to tell me what had happened.

I ran there as soon as I found out about the robbery, crying endlessly. I ran from my house to the shop in my underwear and barefoot because I was so upset, I forgot to even get dressed. I cried my eyes out. They left nothing, those bastards. Not even the chair I sat on when the shop was quiet.

- **"Those bastards", who?**

- Gipsies, of course. The news those days was always about some houses being broken into and places being robbed. Of course, it was them.

My parents were working then, so the first person I called was Emanuele, to tell him what had happened.

- **And what did he say?**

- He got extremely mad, insulting me gravely and yelling things I don't even want to say out loud at me. He told me this was all my fault and that everything had one down the drain.

I tried to defend myself, but he did not have any of it: he said he no longer trusted me, that he never wanted to see me again and that he would keep all the earnings made that week in order to pay for the financial damage, without giving me any money. Then he hung up on me. I tried calling him again, but he never answered his phone again. He never answered any of my calls even after days, weeks and months following the robbery.

The news had been spreading around the town extremely quickly, and what happened to my shop came to my grandma's ears. She died from a stroke in that very moment, and they found her corpse with the telephone still in her hand. I wept a lot for that, too: such a sensitive woman, desperate about what she had just heard.

The police told me I might be right about who had robbed the shop, and told me they would have investigated, though they never got back to me. On the other hand, friends and relatives told me to sue Emanuele, as he was too much of a dodgy person in their opinion. I refused to do so, and I accepted his anger towards me, as well as his decision not to talk to me again.

In the days following my grandma's funeral, I was more and more ashamed of leaving the house. More than anything else, I lacked strength. Therefore, I isolated myself every day more, even spending a full month in bed. I did not want to know anything about vaping and about work. Nothing.

Sometimes I had friends over, but I would tell them to leave as soon as they started telling me that I should stand up for myself and ask Emanuele for the money back. They would also say that my grandma's death was Emanuele's fault. This went on for a while and, in the end, I cut ties with them.

My cousin would visit me often, as we made up following what had happened and he was the only one who agreed not to talk about the deed. He was supporting me, and he was sure that, as he had known Emanuele, it could not have been his fault.

We would spend nights together, smoking joints this huge [*he uses his right hand to point to his left forearm*], then when we got bored, we would go out, though not in Ceprano.

Thanks to him, I started leaving the house again: we went out in towns between Arce and Sora, he would take me to clubs and such. Once, in Arce, I thought I had seen Emanuele in a club, but I must have been a bit too wrecked, bruv.

**- So, did you move to London because you ended up hating your hometown?**

- No, quite the opposite, it was for love. One of those nights I got to know a girl. A dolled-up hottie, who was vaping just outside Grey[5]. Whatever she was vaping on was exactly what I used to sell, it might have been me who sold it to her, since the brand the same.

I told myself that that was a sign, and that I should hit on that girl. So, I got closer to her and told her something along the lines of "I might have sold you that sour cherry flavour vaping pen you are smoking right now, but I do not remember you" and I added "Nice to meet you, I'm Gaetano, the first person who brought vapes to Ceprano".

She looked at me from head to foot and told me "Actually, I bought this in Rome last year", and she left rather disgusted.

I do not even know why or how, but that reply made me fall in love with her so hard. I never saw her again that night, but I

---

[5] Club in the vicinity of Sora, province of Frosinone.

could not stop thinking about that sour cherry flavour coming out of her pulpy lips.

We stayed in the club a little longer because I was my cousin's wingman, who was now kissing some drunk girl. Then after a while we got hungry and the girl suggested we should get something to eat at a nearby McDonald's. So, we grabbed our stuff, left the club, and jumped in the car – with my cousin and the chunky one making out in the backseat – and drove to McDonald's in Sora.

After we arrived, I could not believe my eyes: that hot girl from before was standing there.

We joined the queue at the McDrive, and I started looking at her. She was with some preppy guy looking rich, and they were arguing rather animatedly. At some point this dick slaps her and I lose it completely: I got out of the car and ran to him, slapping this fucking face of his. Like this [*mimicking the scene slapping the air with his arms*].

I smacked this bloody bastard that hard that he ran away with his tail between his legs. You can't even imagine how stocked I was at that point, you just can't!

She goes "Oh but you are the one from the club! Thank you so much", whining like women do, you know.

Then she hugged me and that was it.

I was no longer aware of what was happening around me, I swear, mate. It could have been the most romantic moment ever, but then I realised that my car was at the very front of the queue, and people started honking at me annoyed.

And no, those two animals in the backseat did not even do anything, eh. So, I ran to get back into the car and what did she do? She came with me because she was afraid of that bastard, whom was the boyfriend she had been trying to break up with just then. There was the explanation for that shitty slap he gave her. Damn, if I see him again, I will do him right like Saint Lucia: I will take his eyes out and make him hold them[6].

To sum it up, I ordered some food for the girl as well, who was still visibly shaken. I had read somewhere that eating junk food is good for the soul when you are sad, so I did it gladly. My cousin and the other girl ordered some food as well, blissfully ignoring the fact that someone new joined us in the car, too.

Whilst eating some chick nuggets, she told me with her mouth full "Anyway my name is Martina", and I tried answering but I forgot my name. then, embarrassed I replied, "Nice to meet you, I'm Gaetano" and she said "Yeah, you told me that already" and here we are, in the blink of an eye, my lips were on hers.

She, still with her mouth full, did not refuse the kiss! It was the first time something like this happened with a girl, my heart was beating so fast.

Anyway, what time is it? Oh no, 5.34pm, it is so late, I'm meeting her at 6pm in Leicester Square. Come with me upstairs, so we can finish talking while I get ready.


4


- Come on in, don't be shy. This is my bedroom, it is rather small, but two people can fit in, sit on the bed. Don't mind the cardboard on the floor, my flatmates told me it was put there by the previous tenant. Apparently, he was some Eastern European crackhead who liked to entertain a different lady each night. He left the result of those nights everywhere on the carpet, so the landlady told him to fix the situation before leaving. And he decided to fix it this way.

- **And it does not disgust you, not even a bit?**

---

[6] Saying from Ciociaria, as this Saint was often portrayed with her eyes in her hands.

- Nah, that cardboard protects me. And then this situation fits me perfectly: I only pay three hundred and eighty pounds a month for a single room in zone 3, such a stroke of luck for me, considering that the average single room in this area is around five hundred pounds per month.

Surely, something that bothers me are the paper-thin walls. Just next door there is a couple of Greeks who get extremely loud when they are together, and I hear everything. Ew.

- **And you do not do the same with Martina?**

- No, Martina has never been here. We never did anything of the sort because she says she is not ready yet. I get her, after a year and a half together it is still a bit early for that.

Look at this [*he points to the white shirt he is buttoning up with a smug face*], a friend of mine got this for me. Her name is Serena, she is from Treviso but has been living in the UK for ages. She works at Primark, the one in front of Tottenham Court Road station. She said she stole it, but I don't believe her, she is a good girl deep down.

Poor thing, she works strange hours... You know, she often comes see me at the restaurant.

Anyway, I was saying: Martina and I fell in love in the McDrive lane, and we have started going out and knowing each other better. At the time, she was finishing secondary school - as she is around a year younger than me. She is the daughter of a very popular dentist in our area, in Ciociaria, if you know what I mean.

She was about to finish school, but she has always been very determined: she was going to study English literature at a University in London. She has always been resolute, and I do value her for that.

She was the reason why I stopped playing videogames every day, especially because she kept me busy: every morning I would pick her up from her house and drive her to the school, and then back home. I would help her with Physics and Maths homework which she hated - not that I was all that smart, but internet helped me so much - and often I would take her to her friends' house or shopping.

That has been probably the best time of my life. It is so true what they say: as soon as an awful period of your life ends, an amazing one starts. This has been the case for me.

[*We leave the house and start walking toward the Underground*].

We were always a team. When she was taking her finals, I was right below her classroom's window, telling her the translation of the Latin piece she had to translate. Unfortunately, I got the wrong one, and she held a grudge for a month or so.

You see, she knew that she already had been accepted for a place at Goldsmiths' University, and I had been telling her that I would have loved to move to London with her.

However, because of that tiny mistake I made during her finals, she started telling me that she no longer wanted anything to do with me, that maybe a long-distance relationship was for the best.

But I told her that no, everything she was saying was wrong and that I would have crossed the Thames myself if that was what she wanted.

**- Why the Thames?**

- That river between France and England. The Thames. Wake up pal, geography is not your thing, is it?

Look [*he points to a corner not too far away, covered in flowers and pictures*], do you see all those flowers close to the cinema? They stabbed some guy to death last week. Gang war.

Brawls are everywhere here; you can't even imagine. There have been so many flowers up until some days ago, that I decided to sneakily steal a bunch of roses that were on the wall just there, and I brought them to her. She did not like them, but luckily, I did not tell her that I had stolen them from that corner, or she would most likely have thrown them back at me.

Anyways, I convinced her in the end, and last year around September she left for London and I followed her a couple of weeks later.

Let me tell you, it was not easy. She could not put me up as she lives somewhere in Greenwich whose landlord bans any overnight guests. So, I had to sleep in a hostel in zone 4, North West London, for around ten days.

I told myself that I had to look for a job and proper accommodation those days, also because I did not bring much money with me.

[*We are now in the station and we jump on the first train that comes*].

Every day I would wake up at 4am in that damp, in a room with twenty people, surrounded by mould and cobwebs. Thankfully, they only charged eleven pounds a night, basically a luxury.

Without knowing anyone, I started handing in my CVs to any shop, bar, and restaurant I could find. Every day I would walk around twenty or thirty miles to hand these resumes in. You know, they are a bit behind here, they like paper CVs rather than something emailed to them. The few who got back to me told me they were not looking for anyone.

So yes, this was my routine for the first, second, third, fourth, and fifth day. Then, by the sixth I started despairing. I kept asking myself "Why is nobody getting back to me?!", then I realised that the contact number I put on those CVs was not English. I forgot to write that number, even though I had a working SIM and everything on my phone already, which I got sent when I still was in Italy before I left: English people are so organised when it comes to this stuff, you don't even know.

But nothing happened anyway. Then it came to my mind that some guy from school lived in London and I wrote to him. Not only did they tell me that he was still in London, but he also told me that the restaurant he was working in was looking for new staff. Of course, I offered myself for the position.

The following day I went in for the interview and they hired me on the spot because I probably impressed them, and after then I started looking for accommodation as well. But here is when luck did not help me: after seeing a couple of rooms, I found this shared double room around Walthamstow in that house full of Italians - the one I was telling you about earlier on.

The lettings agency asked for my bank details on behalf of the landlord, but I did not have a bank account at the time, because to open one you must have an employment contract. But then again, to have that employment contract I had to have a bank account. It was a proper Catch-22 situation which was making me crazy.

I went to a few bank branches asking to open a British bank account but due to some Brexit implications, they were not able to help me, as I had no job and no accommodation. Rather desperate, I went to see Martina one night, asking for help. Although she initially tried to send me away, she then introduced me to her flatmate, a guy from Lucca who had been in London for longer than her.

This guy, named Lorenzo, told me that some friends were working in some financial start-ups and he told me to open a bank account using one of these apps. He saved my life.

I have been friends with Lorenzo ever since.

By the way, he should be with Martina right now. Maybe I can introduce him to you.

He was the reason why I managed to get that employment contract - which is a bit fake, mind, but we don't really tell people as technically I'm in the United Kingdom illegally - and as a result the house contract, too. He was a godsend.

Since then, my London life has started: so many other things have changed, I might tell you about them in the future, also because we need to get off now. We are here.

[*We get off the train and we walk toward Leicester Square Underground's exit*].

Migration trends from Italy date back to the Roman Empire, a time when many arrived and settled in Britain under imperial rule.

Over the centuries, this trend increased so much that - according to historian Michael Wyatt - a tiny but influential Italian community started to leave a mark on the rising British Empire, during the Tudor period.

1

- They should be in front of the casino, but I just can't see them…
Ah yeah, Lorenzo is over there!
LORENZOOOOOOO!! LORÈÈÈÈÈ!! WE ARE OVER HERE! [*He starts to wave*].
I don't think he can see us, though.
LORENZOOOOOOOOOOOOOOOOOOOO!!!!
**- It is just so crowded, Gaetano, I do not think he can hear you. Shall we go meet him instead?**
- Yeah, you are right, let me send him a voice message, so that he can start walking towards us.
I can't understand why Martina is not with him…
[*Gaetano starts recording a WhatsApp voice message*].
Yo you *stronzo*[7], turn, we are just behind you. Cross the road.
"Yo you *stronzo*, turn, we are just behind you. Cross the road".
[*The phone repeats*].
- I like listening to all the voice messages I send. It feels like I'm sending them to myself when I actually send them to other people.
LORENZOOOOOOOOOOOOOOOOOOOOOOOOOOOOOOOO OOOO!!!!
I think he saw us. [*Lorenzo crosses the road*].
< What the fuck are you shouting for, stupid. You are late.

---

[7] Italian expression, similar to "asshole". Literally, "a floating piece of shit".

- Shut up crazy, that is not true.
< Well, it is 6.27pm, we were supposed to meet half an hour ago.
- If you are thirty minutes late in Italy, you are on time.
< Maybe around your areas, yeah. We are in London now if you have not noticed. Who is the guy with you?
- Jesus Christ Lorè, chill out. Anyway, he is the journalist, Marco, the one I was telling you about the other day…
- **Well, technically, not yet. Before I can myself a journalist, I must get my Italian press card. Well, also because it is illegal to refer to someone as a "journalist" without this badge.**
- Who cares about these formalities. Let us call yourself journalist and stop being silly, come on. We are in the United Kingdom.
< Ah yes, Gaetano told me about this project of yours. Nice to meet you!
- **My pleasure.**
< From Tuscany as well, yeah?
- **Yes, but I try not to show it too much.**
< Fair enough, also because "Tuscany devastated this country".
- **What do you mean?**
- What country?
< Boris! Come on, the Italian tv show. It's a quote!
- Ah, he is starting with his posh stuff now. Lorè, nobody cares about your shitty tv series.
< It is definitely not shit.
You are shit, such an illiterate caveman, a beggar, and an addict.
- I promise, I have a few flaws too [*he winks at me*].
< To be honest, I do miss Tuscany a bit… But I am not missing the food, or the wine and even good oil. I do not even miss the views, the fresh air, and good steaks, no: I miss bus stops.
- Bus stops?

< Well yeah, because a few Underground stations here have funny names: Seven Sisters, Elephant and Castle, Cockfosters, Wapping. They are… rather naive names, let me put it this way. In Tuscany on the other hand, they take names to a whole new level: Via dei Marmi Distrutti in Culo dal Fascismo e Ricostruiti dalla Resistenza, Madonna Santissima delle Carre del Budello, Via del Puledro Sgozzato in Onore alla Beata Vergine Maria, Ristorante "La Braciola" Forno a Legna 98, Via Sdrucciolo dei Cipollini, Via del Guercio Lercio, and so on and so forth.
I mean, do you hear them? They are angrier… A bit more substantial.
- Wow, we don't even have buses.
< Oh, come on, do not exaggerate…
- No, I'm actually serious. It is not a coincidence that by the age of twelve we can drive our grandparents' tractors, and the wealthier can drive their parents' cars.
< And nobody ever thought of stopping you?
- You ask way too many questions.
Where is Martina though?
< She has to study; she is maybe going to join us later on…
- She did not tell me anything…
< She told me to tell you.
Do not act all offended now.
- Whatever.
So, what are we doing, beer?
< Yes, we can grab one in a pub nearby.
- Not sure if you got the point, we are going to an off-licence and just get on with it.
It was my idea to grab a beer.
< Well I am not drinking whatever crap you drink.
- Then just get yourself a Ribena, or Fanta Grape or Cherry Cola and stop being a pain in the ass.
< I am going to the pub; you can suit yourself.
- I'm only coming if you are buying me a beer.

< You are nothing but a leachy freeloader.
Yeah, that is fine, I am buying Marco one as well.
[*We start walking towards Soho and along the way we stop at a pub*].


2


- I'm getting the next round!
< This is what you always say before you leave, man. So, I am not going to believe you this time.
- Ah, he just knows me too well... [*we sit at a nearby table holding our beers*].
- **Thank you so much for the beer.**
< Not a problem at all...
Careful when touching the table, these Brits are just so dirty, you can't imagine.
- Ah yeah, [*he shows us how his hand gets stuck on the table due to the previous unwashed dirt*].
< So, Gaetano said that you are writing something about Italians in London, is it true?
- I reckon he should be the one asking questions.
< You are so annoying.
Do not mind him, he gets as drunk as a Venetian grandpa at 9am after a few sips of beer.
- What do you even know about Venetian people?
< What do you mean what I know about them, I studied in Padova, I must have told you this a dozen times already.
- Why, is Padova in Veneto?
< Gaetà... [*he looks at him compassionately*].
Look, there is a karaoke just in that corner. Ask them if you can sing a song and just stay there. Beast.
- Wow, I did not notice it! I will go as soon as I finish my beer.

< Beh che ti posso dire, Marco. Cosa vuoi sapere?[8]

I am twenty-five, I live in Greenwich with his girlfriend [*he looks at Gaetano*], in a decent flat we share with a Scottish couple.

I reckon we are quite lucky in that sense.

After finishing a Masters' degree in International Relations in Rome, I was unemployed for a few months until I found a job here, in London, as a *sales specialist* for the Southern European market in a start-up.

It is really not my field, but I get by. To be honest, I am there just to mess up everything these days…

- Wait, is this something new?

< Yeah, as a matter of fact it is something that I wanted to share with you tonight. I will tell you later.

It is not the first thing I change jobs, but we live in London so who cares, there are plenty of jobs here.

- Can you tell me why you want to quit?

< Gaetano, when you drink you get so annoying.

- I'm always annoying.

Whatever, I'm just going to go sing now, bye! [*he gets up and walks to the karaoke stand*].

**- Is he really drunk after just one beer?**

< Yes. I am not sure what is wrong with his body, but he gets drunk really quickly. Well, just you look at how skinny that guy is, he must weigh around fifty kgs or so.

**- Crazy.**

**But yeah, going back to what we were saying, what other jobs did you have?**

< Quite a few.

You know how it is, you graduate and then you look for a job related to whatever you studied.

During my Undergraduate years - in Padova, as I said earlier - I studied Political Science: I would have liked to work as a

---

[8] Italian for: "Well, what can I tell you, Marco. What do you want to know?".

mediator, some sort of peace man. I had been obsessed with this since my high school years, where I studied History, the post-war period, NATO and the UN, globalisation and all that stuff.

It was fascinating for me to think that after endless wars among numerous civilisations, we finally got to the point where we were able to build a social security system, so that these wars could never repeat themselves.

I know, it was nothing but utopian and wishful thinking, considering that wars nowadays are everywhere, and they are even more heinous and violent than the ones in the past centuries. Weapons are much more effective, and the goal is to systemically target the poorest countries by stealing their core values and substitute them with years-long investments, which will generate a capitalistic system. Eventually, this has been why we now have peace: through war. Once inside this world, thanks to my first internship, I was able to assist small and bigger mediators and intermediaries in Rome.

The only drawback was that I did not have a salary, all they gave me were meal vouchers, and this was a problem because Rome is such an expensive city. However, I kept telling myself things like "Well, maybe if I keep on going, I will be able to get some money back". Or "I really hope that all these efforts I have been putting into my work will be fruitful one day".

The hard truth was that I would spend eight, ten - sometimes even twelve - hours a day slaving away for slimy men, bringing cups of coffee to them and their assistants – and lovers - and fixing mundane issues such as installing a piece of software or finding some document in their messy computer desktops.

I was barely surviving, yeah.

I will never understand why people call these "internships" when they are nothing else but exploitation. I am aware that I should have refused all this from the start, but when you start out in your career you know that you will have to put in a lot of hours of work and make sacrifices. The problem was that the more willing I was to put into practice what I had studied at university, the more they wanted to silence me and keep me in my place. I could not do much, as I had found that role thanks to my university network. To make ends meet, I started working as a waiter in the evenings, in a restaurant nearby. Instead of sleeping, I spent my nights wondering whether the path I had chosen was the right one, wearing myself down and repeating to myself that it was not worth it. I felt used and ridiculed. Nothing else but a drop of slime in a society which was basically shitting on my dreams.

After the sixth month of my internship, when they should have started paying me an actual salary and giving me more responsibilities, they told me they were not in a position to pay me yet, all they could offer were the usual meal vouchers.

After that, I started dropping their bags into puddles on purpose, spitting into their lovers' coffees and messing about with their already extremely slow computers. While I was trying to let the air out of one of my bosses' moped - some guy who was convinced that I was responsible for throwing away some of his documents - I got busted. What really happened was that his assistant/lover did that, after finding out that "the genius" started going out with a younger and prettier woman than her. All this without the wife suspecting anything, so funny.

Eventually, they let me go and I accepted it.

Since that day, my mantra has been that I must be respected. I told myself that, considering my education level, a Master's degree would have been ideal for me at that stage of my life. I ended up getting in debt by applying to an International Relations degree in one of those posh universities, only attended by rich Roman kids living in the northern side of the capital. I told myself it had to be worth it in the end. I kept working at the restaurant in the meantime and I was lucky because I loved everyone I was working with, and it is not something you can take for granted.

It took me almost two years to finish my studies. After all those efforts, I felt invincible after graduation.

< Lorenzo, this is for you! *[Gaetano's turn at the karaoke had come]*.

< Oh no. He drank another beer. After two beers he is completely gone.

- *Ladies and Gentlemen, good evening.*

*I'm Gaetano and I'm going to sing a song from my country, Italy.*

*["Happy Birthday"'s tune starts. Behind Gaetano there is a big screen showing the song's lyrics].*

*TANTI AUGURI A TE*

*TANTI AUGURI A TEEE*

*TANTI AUGURI, LORENZO*

*TANTI AUGURI A TEEEE*

*TANTI AUGURI LORENZO, SEI UN GRANDE.*

*[The people in the pub starts clapping their hands and looking at Lorenzo].*

- **Wait, is it your birthday?**

< No. What a retard. *[Lorenzo seems visibly embarrassed by the loud clapping and starts looking at Gaetano angrily].*

*[Gaetano gets off from the karaoke stand, but he trips over the microphone cable and falls awkwardly on a table in front of him, tipping it over. The beers on top of it get thrown in the air and the guys at that table got so mad that one of them pushed Gaetano away as soon as he got back up].*

OH MATE, CAZZO FAI. I PUT THIS MIC IN YOUR BUTT.

< Marco, ignore him, look elsewhere.

*[Gaetano tries to punch the guy, but somebody kicks him on the floor. The Brit tries to jump him, but Gaetano quickly gets up and runs away, leaving the pub. The guy sits back at his table and laughs about the matter with his friends, while tidying up*

*the mess. All the other people in the pub remain indifferent, as if nothing happened].*

< Anyways, I was determined to walk into the world of international politics and ready to stand up for myself…

- **Wait for a second, should not we go check on Gaetano?**

< Do not worry.

He is a fighter. It is also not the first thing that this happens. Let us just finish the beer and then we can go check on him, come on.

As I was saying.

Eventually, I spent the whole summer sending out CVs, day and night. I was sending so many out that the whole thing almost became a full-time job. The disadvantage of my Master's degree was that no internship was guaranteed at the end of it, it was your problem to sort after graduation.

LinkedIn showed over five hundred applications sent out. I tried sending them to companies in Rome, Padova, Milan, even Brussels. Anywhere.

After a month, the only responses I received were automated replies informing me that they did not select me for the position. This is when I started getting upset.

Every day I thought that, if I could have had a pound every time they rejected me for a position, I could have had Elon Musk cleaning my shoes using his ass.

How the fuck was it possible that despite a degree, an apprenticeship and a Master's degree nobody wanted to hire me? What could I do?

I tried writing cover letters, improving my CV a million times. I was so desperate that I tried handing them in personally at various embassies. Nothing came out of it. Not even a phone call. There were a few times where I was able to gain some work experience. You know those situations that make you heave a sigh of relief and make you say "ah, finally!". Well, I had a couple of those.

However, after a few weeks I could tell whether they would have eventually paid me or not. All this while I was constantly working, sometimes even putting extra hours into my job, and at the end all they could say was something like "You know that salary we agreed on when you started? Well, we can't give it to you".

I even stopped answering, I was no longer mentally strong enough to reply to these people. I would leave the following day without explanation. I avoided smashing stuff around because I did not want any trouble.

And this is how I went back to sending out CVs all day long. I felt as ill as a gambling addict. I was totally addicted to this evil and tragic game, which was all about the fading of hope, something that eats you alive and prevents you from doing anything else.

I was so sick and tired of it. And anger was slowly destroying all the hope I had left in myself, every day a little bit more.

The more all this went on, the more I hated academia and the route I chose to take. I was so sure that universities were nothing else but exam factories, where everything was about money, and where nobody gave a shit about students' career prospects. Let alone what happened in that internship I told you about, I was literally a slave.

And to think that I idealised academia so much. I felt abandoned and completely disappointed.

I reached a point where I would not write about my Master education on CVs, convinced that being overqualified would scare potential employers away.

And the icing on the cake was that time where some health officers arrived unannounced at the restaurant where I was working. They found a dead rat somewhere buried in the kitchen, behind the stove. They sealed the place, and the family running the business told me they were unlikely to open again in the future. So, I found myself jobless just like that, at the snap of a finger.

That was the last straw. I was exhausted: I was killing myself to run after some dream that was not even mine anymore, and then there I was in this sticky situation. I told myself I should go home, back to Lucca. Just for a few days, to think more clearly. I waited for a few days and then I convinced myself that I simply could no longer keep living like this. I needed something else, somewhere that would value my knowledge, where I could be at the very least useful.

I applied for some jobs in London, as I got sick of staying in Italy, too.

Out of all those people around my age who remained in Italy, around three out of twenty managed to get their dream job. The rest of them does not study or work, can you believe it? Only those who decided to move to a bigger city made it somehow, but those who stayed in Lucca had no chance. Nothing at all.

Have you ever heard of the book *"Teoria della Classe Disagiata"*, by Raffaele Alberto Ventura? It got recently released, and it was so interesting to read about the author's take on this endless limbo we find ourselves in, accounts written really clearly and which I approve, to some extent.

Basically, young people such as ourselves - middle-class born - are experiencing an existential crisis due to the disillusionment from the economic boom onwards. This crisis was fuelled by the impoverishment of the Western world. To sum up the book - after chatting endlessly about socioeconomic topics - Ventura states that we are experiencing some sort of symbolic capital's over-accumulation, meaning that too many people want to do a certain job once adults, and that unfortunately there are not enough jobs for each one of us.

Like many others, I was myself a victim of this system, too. "What a cutie, he wants to save the world by ending these conflicts with world peace!", bullshit. A dream born out of nothing.

Some sort of ingenuity driven by an engine that feeds on self-imposed thoughts, influenced by a large number of good reads and so many good films I fed myself over the years.

This was the reason why I threw myself onto some completely different sectors - which I had no knowledge of - and I have never been more ready and motivated since. After five days sending CVs around, to random companies, I was contacted by a coffee chain. The owner himself called me up, a man from Aprilia who had moved to London in order to follow his dream. He helped me move to the city, suggested I contacted some of his friends to find accommodation, he helped me with some documents I needed to get in order to work. I trusted him, he told me he would have paid me decently - a thousand five hundred pound a month - and in exchange I would have had to help him fill out various documents to open other shops in town. I thought I had hit the jackpot.

At the end of the day, it was a dream for me: I finally had found a way to become independent without slaving away for fifteen hours a day. Mind, before looking for a job, I said to myself that I would have never worked with Italians once in London.

Quite a challenge, to be fair: you can always fight against this condition, but you can do nothing about this. There are too many Italians here, and anywhere you may be in London, you will always find some Italian person who will notice you and who will try their best to stay around you. And then, when there are no Italians around you, you start missing them rather inexplicably.

I was such a dreamer. I should have followed my instincts of denial and refusal and hold on.

Anyways, once arrived I met him, and I started working for him the next day. There was some sort of gut feeling, you know. And then one afternoon he told me something like: "You should do me a tiny favour, the European Union has this certain ban, and you should apply on your behalf, even if it is actually a project which will be implemented in our coffee shops. We really must act now otherwise once all the Brexit stuff kicks in, we will get screwed over".

Initially, I did not think much of it, and I accepted gladly. But later on, I realised that I would have had to trick the European Union and the money that would have come out of that fraud, would have been used to pay for my salary. I got ripped off once again, essentially.

However, this time it was not the time nor the place to cry, I simply could not afford this. So, I pretended to do this "tiny favour", whilst looking for a new job.

I managed to secure five interviews in ten days: I do not even know how, but apparently, they were all looking for someone with my qualifications. I got selected by some small tech companies, those ones which make apps for services and for retail.

I left that dickhead last-minute, telling him I would have had to go back to Italy for personal reasons. I should have reported him, but I did not. I just felt so very sorry for him. I promised myself that from that day onwards, I would really have had to abandon Italians to their sad fate. I moved and I found this room in Greenwich, then I went for a job at the company I am working at right now: what they do is basically buying vinyl records that no longer fit warehouses and then pack them all up and send them over to hipsters all over the world, who buy them eagerly, hoping to find that life-changing record.

They needed someone multilingual to work as a buyer, as well as someone to work as a salesperson to deal with the administrative stuff. I applied for both roles and they hired me. I get a rather respectable salary now, that sort of money that allows me to live in London decently, I would say. But what I lost is my soul, my aspiration, my ideals.

I keep asking myself whether this is what you are supposed to feel once you are an adult. Or perhaps I am yet to find this out, I am not sure.

Now I just keep repeating to myself that I am happy, when I do not believe I am, is all. It is like there is this big black hole, which is slowly devouring me from the inside, here, feel [*he takes my hand and places it between his sternum and his stomach*]. Do you want to know what the worst is? When I think about my condition, I tell myself that there is no way out, that I did my best. And therefore, I am living this condition as if it were a punishment, aware of all this. I feel in exile, exiled from the place where I was born and raised, as well as from myself.

So, you know what? I should stop feeling this sorry for myself, and I should make peace with this situation and accept it for what it is. Maybe I just need a dog, or a new phone, or perhaps simply a holiday, to stop thinking and bury these thoughts in gin tonics.

You know, it feels like I am still fighting. Somehow, I feel stressed even after years of trying to look for my place in this world. London allows you to be whoever you want. If you end up jobless, you can find another job in no time. This is a double-edge sword if you think about it, shocking and devastating at the same time. You need to become some sort of human chameleon, perhaps even denying your nature to please your potential employer. How exactly can you even be yourself, when your identity still lives in some dead and gone idealisation? I chat about this with Martina quite often. She tells me to keep following that vision, but she does not even know how much I suffered. I do not want to feel like that again. So here we are, aware that our identity does not depend on the job we do, but on who we are. Aware that at the end of the day, the times have changed and that we can't follow the footsteps of our parents, who devoted themselves to their jobs and nothing else.

Our generation is disenchanted and hollow. Gaetano is right, you know, he is right to only follow his heart and believe in love, that is the only thing that counts when all is said and done.

- **Lorenzo, your story is incredible, I am so sorry for what you experienced.**

**Gaetano asked why you want to quit your job, is it because of this, then?**

< Not really. But I think the time has come to check on that poor thing.

[*We get up and leave the pub, looking for Gaetano*].


3


< Jesus, Gaetano, this is disgusting.

[*We find him on the pavement next to the pub, with his vomit all over his shows and spit on his face*].

- He hurt me so badly.

< That guy? Yeah, we saw him.

- No, drinking two beers and smoking that roofie before going out.

< Eh, you must lie in your bed the way you made it.

- Well yeah, I know…

< Well, how my grandma said, "*per i malati c'è la china e per i coglioni non c'è medicina*[9]".

- What does "*china*" mean?

< Good question!

Come on, weirdo, let us take you to the metro.

- Yes, okay. Ooooy [*he gets up with difficulty*].

Really, though, what does "*china*" mean?

< I do not know, Gaetano! [*He starts to get pissed off now*].

- Eh, come on now. Mate, chill out!

---

[9] This is a Tuscan saying. Literally, "For the sick there is cinchona and for the jerks there is no medicine".

[We start walking toward Piccadilly Circus' Underground station].
< Gaetà, do you want some water? You still look way too drunk.
- Shut up, crazy!
[He thinks about it].
Yeah, thank you.
[Lorenzo goes into an off-licence whilst Gaetano and I wait for him outside].
- Why do they keep the lights on in these empty offices? Look at all these buildings with the lights on, what a waste of electricity…
**- I think it is to scare thieves off.**
- Nah, no thieves. Again, the questions never come from you, and your answers are pathetic. What kind of journalist are you, come on, fake newwwwws!!!
< What is happening?
Take this water, drink like animals do [he throws the water bottle to Gaetano].
- Nothing, nothing.
Anyway, what about this job? What did they do wrong, why do you want to quit?
< Look, today I was sick of it all already. To be honest, it has now been a few days where I am just so annoyed by everything they do, but today specifically I was so mad that I just could not behave properly.
I was sulking all day; you know the kind of face I pull when something is irritating me.
- Oh no, poor baby [he strokes his head sarcastically].
< It has been days now where my workstation is all messy. It is like someone comes into the office just to ruin my desk, spraying my stuff with weird liquids, throwing the keyboard off the table, and emptying the bin next to my chair on the floor. Anyway, this happened again today, so I started losing it, asking around if anyone knew anything about it.

Let me first say how I deeply hate my colleagues: the guys are the kind of people who squeeze you hand so hard when they greet you, with such a weird grin on their face, just because some digital marketing guru told them to do so. They keep showing off how macho they are, which is so strange, because when you see them on their own, they are nothing but quiet. The girls, on the other hand - not all of them, but the majority - is like they have a different mask on every other day, you never truly know who they are. They look like a copy of a copy of a copy of some other girl.

So, within this context I am the precise one, the annoying colleague, simply because I try to tell them that they could strive for more, they could be much more ambitious, that not being unique is detrimental, and all these things an old wise man would say. Apparently, they are targeting me and trying to shut me up somehow.

For instance, today, one of my managers called me into her office and she told me that I must smile more, that my negativity is influencing the whole office's mood and that I am killing everyone's joy.

So, I asked her "How can I improve this situation?", and she replied simply: "Pretend to be happy", along with one of those fake smiles people like to put on around here. I have never understood why British people think that the happier and jollier you are, the more productive you are, too. I think this is all bullshit honestly, so as soon as I heard these words, I lost my mind.

At first, I did not say anything, then I thanked her for her "enlightening words", I left her office, and I went to the bathroom to shout all the insults that came to my mind, stuff that I had bottled up inside myself since the morning.

Then, I went back to my desk and acted exactly as she told me to, forcing a big smile on my lips and faking positivity all around.

- And what happened in the end?
< Well, now I just feel like quitting and finding something else.
Preferably, some other office with fewer people to speak to.
Actually, I am attending some sort of fair in a couple of days, I
might make the most of it and get to know a few more people
or see whether other companies are hiring at the moment.
- Yeah alright, we really don't give a fuck.
I'm proper hungry. Fancy a kebab?
< Yeah, totally.
- I really don't get people who don't put onions on their kebabs.
< I normally have them put onions on mine.
- Weird that, I thought you were one of those who don't eat
onions in kebabs. And this is why I can't understand you very
well.
< This is because you are not very smart, pal.
- What happened to Martina, though?
< No idea.

Italian migration to Great Britain reached its peak
in the XVIII Century.

It started as a cosmopolitan and cultural trend – marked by
the arrival of monks, bankers, musicians, architects, painters,
and other kind of artists – which slowly became fuelled by the
economy.

After joining the European Union in 1973, Britain experienced
yet another influx, similar to the previous one.

This trend has been slowed down – and in some ways entirely
halted – by Brexit.

**SERENA (~)**

1

~ Normally, when someone asks me how I am, I want to tell them that I feel like shit. But I can't do that because there is no actual reason why I feel like this. If I said, "I feel crap", someone would surely ask me "Why? What is wrong?", and there I would be, trying to give lame excuses about why I feel how I feel, something that would bore to death even the nicest of people. It just would not be very nice. This is the reason why, when people ask me how I am, I just laugh in their face.

**- How did you meet Gaetano?**

~ Gaetano? Ah yes, it is a funny story that one! We met when we were at a TOY gig at Moth Club, Hackney. I was on my own – something that happens quite often especially when barely known bands are involved – so yeah, just before going into the club, I see this guy crunched up on the floor, looking awful.
That night I was wearing my old Dr. Martens, a pair I bought on Depop, and they looked a bit worn out, but I liked them like that. Anyways, I was about to enter the club when this one here starts staring at me and at some point, he loudly says in Italian *"Che scarpe di merda*[10]*"*, looking at my boots. He thought I was British and that I would not have understood him, the fool. So, I snapped back at him saying *"Tua madre*[11]*"* and he got so offended, the poor baby. We started arguing about my reply

---

[10] Italian for: "Those shoes are crap".
[11] Italian saying, which literally translates into: "Your mother". It is used as a common insult.

being too much and how he did not know I was Italian, so I told him that he should avoid saying rude stuff out loud in Italian, as Italians are literally everywhere in London. This is how a great friendship started.

That night we went to the gig together and they kicked out of the place after half an hour, because he started pushing people around even during the slowest tracks.

I do not even know how, but he managed to ruin my night out so badly, that that very night became one of the best I ever had, since moving to London.

**- When did you move here?**

~ A couple of years ago, more or less. I came here with my ex-boyfriend: a runaway like me. We decided to move to London as we were fascinated by English culture, but mainly because we both thought that Treviso sucks.

I am not sure if you know anything about Treviso: it is split into two sides by the Piave river. On the East bank, everyone tries to act like they are from Belluno, on the West side, instead, people play at being from Venice, and all this does nothing but create a condition where, as a matter of fact, people of Treviso do not really exist. Everybody hates Treviso, everyone hates one another in Treviso.

I witnessed riots because of this stuff, just like Los Angeles has its own violent gangs, but rather than shooting one another in the streets, they fight all over the countryside. Sometimes they even show up with bolt cutters trying to defend themselves. You do not even know how many stories I hear about this... Unimaginable.

**- Why have you never liked it? It sounds like an... interesting place.**

~ Well, look, I never felt like it was my place, even if I was born there. My parents are from Albania, those who "came over on an inflatable boat", in the 90's, after the People's Socialist Republic of Albania fell.

My name is not Serena, it is actually Serina. Serina Calidaj. In school, they all called me Serena, so I got used to it and I now use it as my real name.
**- My bad, I did not know...**
**Do you want me to call you with your real name?**
~ No, do not worry. This is who I am now, I am okay with it. I was just sad about the fact that, even before my teenage years, I had to endure constant discriminations, especially by adults. Therefore, I slowly started hating everyone who led me to isolate myself every day more, especially when I was a teenager, when I started liking bands and groups nobody had heard of before.
Yes, I managed to make some friends eventually, but I did not feel close to them whatsoever, so internet came to the rescue and I started spending my days locked in my room, fixing my problems that way.
The last straw was trying to find a job after I was done with school, months and months trying to find any role within the hospitability industry, but they never called me back.
After yet another rejection, I took matters into my own hands and I called back the lady who interviewed me for a receptionist role a while back, and this moron told me she did not pick me as they wanted someone from Italy. I realised that the more I tried to fit in, the more other people will always see me as the "migrant who came here on a rubber dinghy", any time they read my name on a either document or a piece of paper.
As soon as I could, I decided to move to London with this guy I met at a gig at the New Age Club, in the town of Roncade. We moved into this shithole near Mile End, but stuff went south in no time. I found a job after three weeks, whereas he was still struggling even after a month and a half of looking, and this situation was frustrating for both of us.
We would often fight over the smallest things: dirty dishes, expensive food shopping, unmade bed, and all this made us

realise that we were not ready to put up with each other, that it was way too early to move in together. You know, we were not even twenty yet.

We would also struggle with other things, such as food: when I used to ask him if he wanted to go grab some Thai, he would say "I don't know, I have to think about this", and I really can't stand these answers. What the fuck do you have to think about? It is nothing more than lunch, it is not like we are going to Scotland.

In brief, it was clear to me that things were not working out for us, so we decided to break up. I have never heard from him since. Some friends from back home in Treviso told me they saw him in town, so I think it is quite likely that he moved back home.

London is not for everyone. This city is all about energy: if you decide to be positive, London will give you only positives – interesting meetings, or the luck of finding a job in no time – but if your vibes are off, or if you start complaining and being unreasonable, London will give you nothing but misery back. This is something I have learnt over the past few days. London changes you completely, and you need to be able to handle this change, otherwise you can't cope. You can't protect yourself; you can only welcome whatever it gives you.

Wait, what time is it? Damn, my lunch break is over.

Okay, meet me here as soon as I finish my shift and we can go see Gaetano at his workplace.

- **Perfect, see you later.**


2


[*At the agreed time, Serena leaves Primark and we walk toward Gaetano's workplace*].

~ You can't even imagine what has just happened. There was this mum in the fitting rooms with his kid, who must have been either six or seven years old – I think they were Polish, or Eastern European – who asked me to look after him so that she could try on a dozen of those ugly miniskirts to go clubbing or something. So yes, I keep an eye on this child – as the shop was surprisingly quiet – and what does this tiny one do? I do not know how, he started solving a Rubik's Cube he had with him, in around fifteen seconds. I could not believe my eyes, thinking that I was definitely less smart than a toddler, pathetic.

Trying not to think about my miserable life, I started scrolling my phone mindlessly, looking for some fun memes to improve my mood, also because this kid kept showing off and I could not stand him any longer. And then, after a few minutes he goes: "Why are you so glued to that phone, should you not be working?".

And I told him: "Well, love, reality sucks".

He nods at me and as soon as his mum gets back, he starts yelling "REALITY SUCKS!". His mum starts hitting him on the head so badly, that for a while I enjoyed the show, but now that I think about it, I feel a bit guilty. I think there might be a new emo in town thanks to me.

This is to show you that, as you can see, London's energy theory is indeed true: I have always been a bit of a rebel – you know, I am a Capricorn – and this kid represents the idea of what being miserable means in London. Rubbing our limitations in our faces, making us feel terrible.

I really believe in this stuff, you know.

**- Despite this negative energy, do you never think of going back home?**

~ Home? Definitely not, London is my home. I have nothing left in Treviso, and nothing makes me want to go back there. I am happy here.

You know, London does not set any limits, that butthole of Treviso does. Apart from systematic racism, you can't be yourself at the fullest and completely, a bit because of people who are not curious and are content with their lives, and a bit because there is no way for us to develop ourselves and understand what we are made of, no right places and no such incentives.

**- What do you mean by "right places"?**

~ You know, like, places where you can share ideas and improve yourself. Gigs, for example, are perfect for meeting new people. I met Gaetano this way and, let me tell you, I would have never met someone like this in any other circumstance. Obviously meeting this guy at Moth was not intentional, we are very different people: he was not there for the gig, he just wanted to end up black-out drunk. But I do not think that this happened by chance, fate made us meet in that moment. Fate itself generated a kind of energy that I now can feel so pure inside me: Gaetano is a pure soul. It is the end point, but it is also fuel for my soul, which means it is now a piece which makes me, me.

This is what I mean by the "right places", those ones where you can reflect and develop thanks to other people.

**- And do you think that Gaetano thinks the same things about you?**

~ I do not believe this, no. Or rather, he does not think like this just yet. I am not even that sure that he will get to this point.

He is blindly fighting within himself, everything about him is short-term: he is not doing anything in his life, he is not here for himself, he is only here because of his girlfriend. And this girl does not even care about him that much, but he does not seem to mind either.

He is happy with the idea of being loved, even when this does not even exist. As long as he does not realise this, he will be happy in the end. However, you can see that he is struggling with this unknown feeling he has. I only hope that all this will not go against him eventually.

Going back to London itself, do you know what really annoys me about this city? That every road is the same: once you leave an Underground station, what do you see? McDonalds and KFC, Costa Coffee and Starbucks, Subway and Pret A Manger, Nando's and Wagamama. Small businesses are no longer a thing, they are devoured by these soulless retail giants which ruin the scenery – or, better, the soul – making everything look the same.

I do not even trust who buys from these chains. If I am being honest, they properly piss me off.

I do not know if you noticed this but, following the economic crisis, while on one hand many people stopped buying non-essential stuff, many others have instead started buying from these places as they sell cheaper things. On one hand we now have a consumer's paradise, thriving on hatred, on the other what we have is now a jump from a consumeristic to a hyper-avaricious society. These are also the main reasons why the United Kingdom voted Leave in the Brexit referendum, if you think about it.

You know what, though? I think that we have always been a hateful society – and my experience is one of the many examples there are of it – and that buying things all the time was nothing else but a way out, something to keep us quiet. Therefore, when these activities will die out, due to war, a natural disaster or yet another and more powerful economic crisis, we will probably end up with a civil war.

**- I find it weird to listen to these theories by someone who works for a fast fashion multinational company...**

~ Damn you, this is a low blow, man. There is a difference between working for a chain and buying from it.

During my first year here, I worked for a small fashion store, and you have no idea how hard it was, not rewarding and not even well-paid even if I was working full-time hours.

The actual job was just a job. And the shop manager was such a bad person, too.

My wages did not even meet the minimum wage, and I was hired off the books. All those trial periods I had to do were obviously unpaid, I was going mental when the rush hour started in the shop, it was just slavery at the end of the day. Long hours for nothing in return.

To get my first salary, I had to threaten them with going to the police and telling them all about their illegal business. All the workplace bullying I had to endure is still all over the emails I sent to my former colleagues.

I looked for a job in a big chain just so that I could start working legally, being paid at the end of the month, even if the exploitation is still there – day and night – when the night shift kicks in.

I agreed to this just to survive. People addicted to shopping are the ones paying my wages, even though just thinking about them irritates me so much. At the end of the day, I had to strike a compromise with my ideals, just so that I could live freely. I am aware that is sounds contradictory, but I am at peace with myself now. And in spite of everything, I feel sorry for small businesses that are crushed by these big companies, even if even they exploit their own staff.

I often tell myself that I would like to change jobs, maybe even go back to school, but then I realise that I actually do not need this. I am okay with how my life looks like at the moment. I settled for this.

Look, Gaetano's restaurant is just here.

[*We enter the restaurant*].


3


~ Hey tiny squishy kitty poo, what are you up to?

- Hey stinky toilet and hello to you too, Marco. As you can see, I am working [*though Gaetano is actually sitting on a stool, playing Zombie Tsunami*].

~ Yeah, I can see how busy you are. If you want, we can come over later on…

- No, now that you are here, I can offer you a quick coffee. The manager is not around so it is all on the house.

- *Carina la bottega*[12].

- Yes, it was opened by the restaurant next door. People come for a quick bite if they don't fancy a proper lunch, but we also have customers who come here to buy authentic Italian products. As you can see, we have a lot of oils, tuna, pasta, honey. I am in charge of it.

~ You can see how busy it is all the time… [*she winks ironically*].

- Stop it! Sometimes people come. Perhaps around a dozen a day.

~ You are a joke. I speak to that amount of people every half hour every day where I work. Spoilt and privileged. He also gets free meals, this one.

- I mean, that is the minimum they can do. I'm on minimal wage money, while being completely off the books.

~ Oh, poor thing… [*She gets a honey pot from a shelf, opens it, and sticks a finger in it to try and taste it*].

- No, crazy! What are you doing? They are going to kill me if they find out…

~ Shut up, I am taking this home. Tell them you dropped it while cleaning.

- Do you even know that honey is just bees' vomit? A friend's uncle from down South explained to me once, he works with bees.

~ Ew, I am already over this [*she spits the honey back in the pot and puts it back where it was*].

---

[12] Italian for "What a nice little shop, this is!".

Damn you and your country knowledge.
- You simply underestimate nature. Have you ever thought about the fact that it is not us who grows trees and plants, but it is them that grow us, giving us oxygen and food until the day we die, when they can finally feed on us when our bodies are all decomposed?
~ You smoked today, right? [*Serena looks at him frowning*].
- You know me too well, my friend, way too well.
They had me clean some warm period blood on the toilet this morning, I am simply trying to forget it ever happened.
~ Why can't you go back to being a rider, if you hate this job so badly? I would gladly swap with you, you just have to do small jobs around the shop, nobody bothers you really.
- **Did you use to be a rider?**
- Yes, when I had to change houses from Walthamstow. I needed a bit of extra cash to pay for some expenses, and for a short time I became one of those people who brings food to the hungry, people who order food on apps and such.
~ The hungry… What a word. They are ordinary people, not homeless. But, rather, tell him why you quit [*she cackles*].
- No.
~ Come on…
- Okay, okay. [*He sighs*].
There were quite a few complaints about the food I was carrying, which was no longer really edible. Be it due to the backpack which kept falling on the floor thanks to this annoying rain, which is a constant in London, or be it because I would fall off the bike every day for the same reason. So, they banned me from the app because of the amount of negative feedback I received. Bastards.
~ Every single time he tells this story, I laugh so badly, I swear. I imagine him throwing on the floor a bunch of dishes and food and then himself falling off the bike, what a laugh.

- *Ridi, ridi he la mamma ha fatto gli gnocchi.*[13]

You see this scar I got under my chin? [*He shows it to Serena*].

I got it because of one of those falls.

[*Serena starts laughing so much she collapses on the floor in tears*].

~ Someone should really write a book about your life; you are too funny.

**- Why did you leave Walthamstow in the end?**

- Nothing serious, really.

I saw a post on this Facebook page, called "SEI DI CEPRANO SE[14]", by this guy who claimed to have found the perfect method to turn a rough aluminium ball into a perfectly round and smooth one. All you needed to do was to microwave that ball for a minute and it would have got into that amazing shape. It was a Bank Holiday Monday, and I was off work, I was bored to death, so I decided to give that experiment a try. It only took ten seconds for stuff to go mental: the microwave blew up catching fire, and the flames reached the cupboard above, burning both the wallpaper and the countertop. Just like that, super-fast.

It was so dangerous: I almost set the whole house on fire!

After all this, I was panicking, so I got a bucket of water to stop the flames, but I also flooded the other side of the kitchen which was not on fire.

I was not aware that you can't microwave metals and such! I only learnt this after my flatmates told me, when they found out about what had happened with the fire. They also told me that unless I moved out and paid for all the damages, they would have called the police on me.

~ Ah, you are just a misunderstood genius, you.

---

[13] Italian idiomatic expression, which sarcastically invites the interlocutor to keep laughing even when something is not funny.

[14] The town's group on Facebook.

- Obviously, the first thing I did, as soon as stuff calmed down, was to contact the guy who put the pictures on Facebook to insult him and threaten him. He blocked me as well. If I see him, I swear I will kill him.

Then, right after what happened, I started getting asthma attacks, I could not breathe or sleep. I cried so much but I was not even sure why. After a few days I went to the GP, who said that those were panic attacks and that I should try and chill out a bit. I started smoking every day after that. To be honest, I have never felt better lately.

~ Yeah, you can tell. You look terrible.

I think you should give everything up, lock yourself in a monastery at the top of a mountain and start working as one of those wise gurus people like listening to. But, well, unfortunately people are way too prejudiced against who starts a life of contemplation.

I do not know why, but you remind me of an old man I met in Veneto a few years back.

I was going to Bologna in BlaBlaCar[15] for a His Clancyness' gig, and after a while we stopped to get some coffee in Trebaseleghe, some place near Padova in the middle of nowhere. In front of the counter, next to me there was this lovely old man, drinking an Aperol Spritz cocktail at eleven o'clock in the morning, who starts talking to me in a quite intricate local dialect. I smile and nod to be polite, but I do not understand a single thing he is telling me.

You would not say, but there are so many differences between Padova's and Treviso's dialects.

After that, he drowns his drink in four seconds and leaves the place giggling. Such a pity, I would have liked to remain and study this *Übermensch*, to try and find a way to understand his

---

[15] Carpooling app popular all over Europe.

strange language. A bit like *Arrival*, that movie about aliens which came out last year.

Yeah, spending time with you is just deepening the relationship between myself and that old man from Trebaseleghe. The vibes are the same and this stuff is turning me on.

- You are mad.

~ Well, you are, too.

I think I need the toilet. Do you ever happen to stop and wonder about how many people are peeing in the very moment you are peeing, too? I would love to connect with those people through telepathy and get in touch just for as long as it takes to pee, to motivate each other in that short time. No? Never? I always do! Like right now. I am off. [*She goes to the back of the shop where the toilets are*].

- What a moron… [*he whispers*].


4


- **I can sense some sort of feeling with Serena, you know…**

- No, of course now. We are just friends.

- **Yeah, you clearly like each other, that is what I am saying.**

- Well, yeah, that is true.

[*A woman enters the shop*].

- Hey there, can I help you?

= Hi, do you have some hummus?

- No, sorry, Miss.

[*The woman leaves the shop, annoyed*].

- These people are all stupid, what do you expect to find in a deli? Garden stuff?

I would have liked to reply to this woman saying something like "No Miss, I'm sorry, no hummus here, but can I offer some dirt from the garden instead?".

- **Gaetano, hummus is that chickpea spread they make in Arab countries…**

- Is it? I most certainly did not know about it.
Never tried it.
- **You should.**
- Well, I would not know. It looks a bit disgusting. I like Italian food. And kebabs. And McDonald's, too.
I'm not really interested in other countries' cuisines; it looks like they would make me sick.
What a weird lady.
What was she thinking, an Italian deli selling hummus?
This was not the first time that some strange customers came in: a couple of months ago there was this old lady chatting to me about how chemtrails are making kids autistic. So annoying. She took about an hour to explain to me how her nephew became autistic in no time.
- **And you? Why did you not ask her to leave?**
- No, I believe in the chemtrails' theory. The conversation was interesting for a while but then she started talking about her nephew and that bored me.
- **Okay, I see...**
[*Serena comes back into the main part of the shop*].
~ Gaetà, what are you doing tonight? Not sure, I am having dinner here and then just going back home.
Did you have plans?
~ I wanted to go out but then I changed my mind.
- Cool.
~ Cool.
- So, are you leaving? When are we meeting up again?
~ I do not know. Never.
- Sounds good to me.
~ Right, bye guys, kisses!
[*Serena leaves the shop and walks away*].

According to an OECD report, Italy is the eighth most common country of origin for migrants worldwide.

Two thirds of Italians abroad do not come back to their motherland.

# THE RESTAURANT

1


- You should not believe what Serena said, it's not true, she's just crazy. I work so much here. Hell, if I don't! I spend my days cleaning this bloody shop and help out at the restaurant when they need me to. I serve customers who just want a quick bite, and sometimes I just stay there chatting with them.
You know, last week some Brazilian guy working in the City came and – the more and more wine I poured into his glass – I got him so drunk that he left a small bag full of change as a tip. There were around thirty-two pounds worth of coins; can you believe it?
After my shift was done, I spent that money on a bunch of amaryllis, and I gave them to Martina. They are her favourite flowers, as well as tulips. But I can find those in supermarkets for a fiver normally, so I thought that the others would have been a bit more stylish.
She was so happy: we walked along the London river – what's it called again... - and we kissed at sunset, on the top of the Greenwich hill, where the Observatory is! It was insane, it was the first time after New Year's Eve last year. Anyways, a gentle reminder: if you want to take a girl to a romantic location, bring her to the Royal Observatory, not to Primrose Hill. Everyone says Primrose Hill is better, but that is not true: the real view is from Greenwich. You can see Canary Wharf's skyscrapers and they are so close to one another that it looks like America, not England. By the way, do you want to see something cool?

Hold on a second, let me close the shop as nobody is going to come anyway.

[*Sluggish and carelessly, Gaetano moves the outdoor table inside the shop, switches off the outdoor and indoor lights, shuts the door from the inside and uses his hand to show me the way to the backroom*].

[*Suddenly, someone knocks on the front door*].

- We are closed, sorry!

'*Sti rompi coglioni oh*[16]. They always come to bother me at closing, these idiots, and most times they only want a coffee, or to buy the cheapest pasta we have. They never want to buy something that like, for instance, is worth a hundred pounds or so, no, it is always stupid orders at the weirdest and latest time.

[*The man at the door keeps knocking*].

- Nooo, we are closed. Come back tomorrow [*he gestures to leave*].

We should go now, otherwise this one will keep bothering us. Careful on the stairs, they are so steep: this building must be at least two hundred years old, they built everything super tiny back in the day [*I follow him to the back of the shop, to get to the rooftop*].

Here is where I sneakily smoke by myself. I love people-watching from here, from this height. If you stand here, behind that build over there you can see the massive Ferris wheel in front of the Big Bang.

- **I think you mean the Big Ben.**

- Yeah, that one, come on. No need to be so picky, it bothers me.

This is the only place where I feel at peace. Away from everything and everyone. Take this air in! [*He breathes loudly*]. It also looks cleaner than it does when you walk around town or you use the Underground. You really have no idea: sometimes

---

[16] Italian translation for: "These annoying pricks, oh".

I get these black boogers which scare me. Just to let you know how polluted this place it.

Feel how quiet it is! If you can ignore the honks, it is so peaceful.

[*A cell phone rings*].

Oh, it is mine.

Hello?

• Gaetano you are a fucking retard, if you don't open up the shop this very moment, I will smash that shitty face you have, and I will throw boiling Earl Grey tea at it [*I can hear clearly from his phone*].

- On my way!

[*He hangs up and gestures to follow him*].

I understand now why that guy was dying to come in, he was the restaurant's barista, Enrico. Quick, or I'm a dead man.

[*Due to the running, Gaetano slips on a step and falls on the floor awkwardly. I try to help him up, but the pain starts making him go crazy*].

THESE FUCKING OLD STAIRS. OH, MY KNEE. MY GOD, MY GOD. I BROKE IT, I'M SURE OF IT. SWEET VIRGIN MARY HELP [*Gaetano tries to get back up despite the pain, trying not to shout too loud*].

Nah, alright, nothing happened.

[*Gaetano opens the shop's front door*].

• I mean, I knock, and you ignore me?

- Enrico come on, it was so dark, I could not see you.

• Sure, yeah, you are twenty going eighty, you moron.

- This is Marco, he is a journalist who is interviewing me for a couple of days.

- **I am not a journali…**

• Whoa, are you working for RAI?[17]

- **Not really, no.**

---

[17] The Italian BBC.

• Ah, too bad. Gaetà, they told me to tell you that it is dinnertime. *Spaghetti aglio, olio e peperoncino*[18] tonight.
Are you staying for dinner, Marco?
- Yes, sure. Please don't be shy!
*[Gaetano locks the door two-way and we go to the restaurant next door through the back shop with Enrico].*


2


- **How many years have you been here for?**
• Me? Ah, I moved here in 1986. I was about this idiot's age [*he points the fork at Gaetano, and then starts rolling up his spaghetti*].
It has been over thirty years now that I think about it. Sweet Jesus, how time flies. Very, extremely different years than today, totally. How hard you would have had to work back then, not like today. Today everything sucks.
- **Have you always worked here?**
• No, I worked as a carpet fitter in the beginning. For around two years. I would put down flooring in British houses, mainly. I had to stop because the company that employed me went bankrupt due to financial trouble, not even sure what for exactly, though. So, at the end of the day, I have been slaving away in London for around twenty-nine.
You know, this restaurant used to be renowned, back in the day. It was one of the most distinguished Italian restaurants of the area. It was a three-storey restaurant, fully booked every night. I used to serve up cocktails to very famous people, once I even served Princess Diana, can you believe that!
- Yes, what a lion! Even The Beatles, Pavarotti, and Pope Wojtyla!

---

[18] Spaghetti with garlic, oil, and chilli.

• Not really, the Pope and Pavarotti never came here, but The Beatles would come here often, at least that is what they say, as I was not working here back then.

- Swear down?

• Ask Sandro or the boss if you see him. I'm not even joking. I mean, this place was full of famous people in the past. There are still a few who come every once in a while, but it is definitely not like the older times.

There were more than a dozen waiters, three people behind the bar counter preparing Martinis over Martinis and the kitchen was full of people, I can't even remember how many people were working here to be honest with you.

Now there are only four people working in the kitchen, and three are from Portugal. To this day I still can't understand what they say!

In terms of waiting staff, three waiters are too many: there are nights when we don't even have a single customer.

By the way, your friend, thingy… Roberto. What happened to him?

- Who, that guy I went to school with? No idea, I have not heard from him for around a year now. He posts pictures on Instagram of cappuccinos and pastries daily, but I'm not sure whether he is still here or has gone back home now.

Anyway, it is almost like I have more customers in the shop than you have in the restaurant!

• Well, yeah, you are right at the end of the day. We don't even know how long we can keep on going like this. The owner, Mister Maurizio, is ninety-three and is always locked in the party room, watching Chelsea matches.

As soon as he dies [*he touches his crotch for good luck*], we are out of a job, let me tell you. Also, because his kids don't care.

You know who is to blame for this decline, though? Arabs. These bloody shisha smokers. It has been ten years now that around here they keep opening up these Lebanese, Algerian and Egyptian cafes, they pop up anywhere all the time. This used to be a classy area, and they ruined it completely.

And don't let me start going on about cars! This used to be a pedestrian area. Now, due to the small pavements, nobody comes anymore. Nobody takes a stroll around here. Everyone just walks with their faces glued to their fucking phones, stuck all together even when they walk, bumping into one another without even saying excuse me.

Ah, I can't wait to get my hands on my pension, honestly.

[*Suddenly, there is silence in the room, with Enrico and Gaetano looking down to their phones quietly. In the meantime, I look around: there are expensive-looking huge paintings on the room's walls, as well as lush and bright green plants on stands. Both the art and the greenery try to perk up the otherwise desolate scene, with the restaurant not open for business yet*].

• You know what really pisses me off about those people who remained in Italy? They keep sending me those stupid sparkling pictures of Minnie and Mickey Mouse, of roses, angels, and coffee cups with "Good morning" as a caption, or "Good afternoon", "Happy Easter", even when it is not even Easter [*he shows these pictures on his phone*]. And every single time I have to reply, as if I don't, they start sulking! You really need to see my phone gallery; it is full of these pictures and I'm not even sure how to delete them all. Screw all this, really.

- Well, just ignore them, no? [*Gaetano says, gobbling the last spaghetti*].

• Nah, I told you. They get mad. They start telling me I don't love them anymore and that they are not in my thoughts. So, I just keep them, and I send the same images back to them. Wait, why are you not eating the garlic?

- No, you take it [*Gaetano moves what remains of the spaghetti to Enrico's plate*].

You are disgusting, you know.

• *You* are disgusting, garlic is so tasty.
- Oh well. This pasta is amazing, well done, chef! [*Gaetano yells toward the kitchen, with no response*].
Well, I think we should go now. See you tomorrow, Enrì?
• Yes of course. If I don't show up, then I'm probably dead.
- Nice, never change, yeah? Always positive! Cheers.
[*We leave the restaurant, and we walk toward the Underground station*].

3


- You know Marco, at the end of the day I'm happy with this life. I do not have to overwork myself, do not have to work extra hours to get by, I always get paid on time and I have friends, my girlfriend and I have fun all the time when I go out. What can be better? [*In the meantime, he has taken a joint, ready to be smoked*].
This is a ritual for me, every time I finish work, I smoke one of these while walking to the Underground. This time I put a bit of hashish in it to make it extra strong. Give me fifteen minutes and once in Wood Green I will probably have to drag myself home, I will be too wrecked [*he lights it up and starts smoking it happily*].
I'm so happy to have left home when I did: nobody is bothering me – apart from the landlord when I'm late with the rent – and fun friends I always hang out with, doing cool stuff. I can't wait for Martina to graduate and find a job, so that we could move in together and I will be completely satisfied with my life at last. It is the only thing that I'm actually looking forward to.
You know, I think I'm quite different from people my age: I would really like to have kids. Raising them how I want, teaching them Italian when they will have to speak English in school…
- **So, you want to stay here long-term and settle down?**

- Yes of course, there is no way I'm going back there [*he takes a long hit*]. Wow, this is fucking strong [*he coughs furiously*].
I have been in London for over a year. I don't think that I will do as some of my acquaintances have done, they were here for around a month or so, and then they got tired of it all and they decided to go back home. No, there is no reason for me to go back to Italy. Another reason is that I'm still ashamed by the whole vaping shop situation you know, especially when it comes to friends and family.
- **Make new friends, maybe?**
- Ha, in Ceprano? No way, everyone knows everyone. It is impossible to make new friends in a situation like this, in such a small place.
Turn left, we are here.
[*We are about to enter the Underground station when Gaetano's phone starts ringing*].
- Hello?

...

Mmh, when?

...

Is there really nobody who can cover for him?

...

Okay, I'm on my way.
[*He hangs up the phone, huffs, and gestures to go back*].
- Bruv, this is not what I wanted. Sandro has just called me, I mean the restaurant's host, telling me they are one waiter short tonight because in an hour or so Antonio Conte is coming. Yeah, the football manager. It is his wife's birthday, and they booked a table for around ten people. Armando, one of the waiters, is off sick and I need to cover for him.
Please mate, keep me company tonight. You can sit at a table close to me and give me strength, please, I need it.
- **Yes, Gaetano no problem.**

- Thank you, my friend, you are the best! You might not know, but even if I met you yesterday, there is a feeling between us. It is like we have been friends for thirty years. I think you should move to London, as well. We can get a double room, just me and you. We can share it! It would be so nice, you know. I can't stand this fact that you will be going back to Italy, too. I would want to be run over instead. Here, now. But oh well, I can't. I need to go back to work now. Is Antonio Conte the one with the wig? I think I heard the guys from the restaurant talk about him. They only talk about football, those ones. I don't even follow it, it does not entertain me whatsoever, I actually find it rather boring and ridiculous. It is so funny; you should have seen what the general reaction was when Italy failed to qualify for the World Cup last month. They were absolutely desperate, devastated, and heartbroken. They spent two full days shouting "THIS IS SO SHAMEFUL, SHAME! ITALY DID NOT EVEN MANAGE TO QUALIFY, SUCH A PITY. IT IS ALL DISGUSTING. I WILL SUPPORT ENGLAND FROM NOW ON. They were like this. Every hour. You should have seen them. Sometimes, they were just staring in the abyss. Looking at them, it looked like someone they loved died. When my grandma died, I was the same. Well, I would also cry for the robbery at the shop, but I was so sad for my poor nan. It is not fair. Who knows where her poor soul is right now. I believe in reincarnation. Serena told me about this once, she is obsessed with this stuff. Sometimes I hear her voice in my head telling me what to do. Maybe she reincarnated into my brain, what about that? It would be ridiculous, but possible. Sometimes she is the one suggesting me to do things: the other night, when I punched that guy in the pub, it was not my doing. She is the one who told me to do that. I swear down. I can normally hear her when I'm drunk or high, and I often drink and take drugs just to hear her voice. She was the only one who understood me at home. I miss her a lot. Do you want to be my new grandma, Marco?

**- Yes Gaetano, sure. But I think we are now lost.**

- Fuck, yeah you are right. We are on the opposite side of everything. Call an Uber, I can't be bothered walking, I just want to sit down and thank people because they are here with us in this very moment. Since I have been here, I noticed that Londoners do not thank people, have you ever noticed it? When I get off the bus, I always thank the bus driver, sometimes I even try and chat to them, but they just shut me up and tell me to hurry up. As if I wronged them somehow. Since then, I stopped thanking them, they do not deserve it. Such rude people, man. And you could say "Well, they might have earphones on", but then again, I always look out for those. I see them as my friends, I understand them at the end of the day. I would talk to myself all day long if this were socially acceptable. Okay, yes, I see where we are right now. We should go this way; I know this shortcut [*we start going into a muddy and badly lit park*]. don't mind the mud, after you walk on the pavement it will just go away. You know how there are so many squirrels here? Once I tried to feed them some tuna I stole from the shop, but I think it was not good for one of them, the poor thing. It started making weird sounds, such as those cats make when they are about to throw up. I was so sorry. I wanted to take it to a vet, but I was in such a hurry, I was on my way to a karaoke night with Martina and Lorenzo. Why do I never do anything right? I feel so useless sometimes. It is such an awful feeling. I mean, I always try hard, but at the end of the day I either hurt someone or I break something. I'm thirsty. Sometimes that really pisses me off about London is that there are no drinking fountains around. It is such a tragedy. You always need to buy bottled water. Which is such a scam, because once the water is finished, I never know what to do with this bottle in my hands. I want to bin it, but after the terror attacks a few years back, they removed all the bins from the streets of the town centre. And so, you have this bottle, and when you find a bin to get rid of it, the bin is overflowingly full, because everyone has the same issue. Careful, though, there is another problem: peeing. Where can you pee in London when there are no public toilets anywhere? I use trees or dead-end alleys, but when I can't do so, I end up having to go one of those independent cafes where businessmen and hipsters buy stuff they don't need, pretending to work on their laptops, just to use the toilet. It is a proper a Catch-22, as you can see. A vicious circle where, to meet your basic needs, you need to keep paying. And how do the poor homeless do? There are so many over here, poor them. Sometimes I give them the expired tuna I sell in the shop, also because I feel sorry throwing it away. They always thank me with massive smiles on their faces. They tell you those products are expired, but it is not true: it is just a trick to make you buy more tend more tuna as soon as possible. The first months here I ate so much expired tuna, and I was fine. It is such a shame that there are so many homeless people around, they don't deserve this, anything they might have done in their lives, they did not deserve to end up sleeping in the streets. Well, it will probably be my case when Martina and I break up, hoping that this will never happens [*we get to a road, and see the restaurant in front of us*]. Well, we are here now. I told you it was a shortcut. Sorry if I spoke so much, when I'm high, I just start chatting no-stop. So, I think I'm pretty high. Oh no, how the hell am I supposed to work now?

4

¤ You took your time, pal! Come on, go get ready, they are coming in ten minutes!
- Good evening to you too, Sandro. Could I have a glass of water please? You are awesome, your hair looks amazing. Well, fully booked tonight as well, I can see! [*The dining room is empty, with only a waiter preparing the tables*].

¤ Stop being a moron. Look at your shoes! Take them off immediately, both of you. You, too! Come on, quick!
- Sandro, he does not work with us, he is a friend of mine.
¤ I don't care, take your shoes off right now, I have just finished moping the floor!
- Okay, mummy [*we start walking barefoot to the locker rooms on the first floor of the restaurant*].
Every time I talk to him, it is like speaking to some girl with PMS: he just shouts at you, for no reason. So annoying.
• Ah, you are back here! [*Enrico appears while walking down the stairs*].
- Hello, pretty lady. Yes, they called me back because of the famous guest.
• Wow, break a leg! Do you want a few eye drops? You look lost.
- Yes, that would save my **ass**. Come here, let me give you a kiss.
• No, mate, please. Go look into my locker, it is right there.
- You are the best, I love you, Enrì.
• *Statte accort, guagliò*[19].
- Yeah, take it easy friend!
[*Once in the dressing room, Gaetano starts using the eye drops found in Enrico's locker, he gets undressed and changes into clean waiter clothes, probably not his. He does all this whilst humming Despacito*].


5


[*Back in the main room – with clean shoes myself, albeit three sizes larger – I sit at a table not too far from the one Chelsea's manager is sitting at, after Gaetano ordered me to pretend to*

---

[19] Colloquial Italian dialect to say: "Be careful, pal".

*do something. As I cannot stay next to him while he works, I will write here what he reports to me.*

*Once Mister Conte arrives with his wife, his daughter and a few more guests after them, Mister Maurizio, the owner, welcomes them. They all look rather elegant, especially the birthday woman, who is wearing a long silky dress with a low neckline on the back.*

*Apparently, Mister Maurizio is a hardcore Chelsea fan, as he welcomed them all while wearing a Chelsea scarf on. I cannot hear what they say due to the distance, but it looks like that they have known each other for a while.*

*Gaetano is now on the other side of the room, away from the main door and close to the table to prepare the last things, despite the evident difficulty he was experiencing to place the balloons next to the party. The other waiter goes up to him, probably to stop him, but this does not stop Gaetano from doing what he wanted to do. A rather loud argument starts: the guy tries to move the balloons, but Gaetano does not give them up and in an effort to grab them from his colleague, he tries to turn around. However, the other waiter inadvertently makes him trip on the floor, making Gaetano fall and the balloons fly to the ceiling. Those balloons were now destined to remain stuck there, due to the very high ceiling.*

*On the other side of the room, it looks as if nobody noticed the argument and the guests – busy chatting among themselves – sip on the cocktails Enrico has prepared at the bar.*

*Gaetano, now back on his own feet, seems unbothered by the whole situation and he cannot stop looking at the balloons on the ceiling, anxious. Once sat at the table, Conte and his guests look surprised by these floating objects above their heads, showing appreciation for such a friendly welcome.*

*Gaetano, looking smug, volunteers to pour the guests some prosecco: he starts with the football manager, ignoring the general rule that women should be served first, especially if she* is the celebrated. This was definitely not overlooked by Mister Conte, who starts telling Gaetano off first by looking at him viciously, and then telling him directly. "Women first, women first!", he tells Gaetano with a high-pitched and ringing voice. Gaetano seems to be giving signs of understanding and sadness, so he tries again by pouring some prosecco into Conte's ten-year-old daughter, thinking he was doing a good thing, as he was starting to serve women in order of age. Unfortunately, this was also something to be reprimanded for, and whilst the other waiter brings some fish antipasti to the table, Gaetano is promptly insulted.

"I'm so sorry Mister Conte, but I am dyslexic" I can make out from the movement of Gaetano's lips while he tries to pour the last drops of prosecco in the remaining glasses, showing regret for the misunderstanding. Then he looks in my direction and winks at me.

In the meantime, Gaetano's actions catch Sandro's eyes, who is standing in a corner of the room making sure everything goes as planned. When the waiters take away the finished main courses from the table, Sandro tries to intercept Gaetano to try and tell him something. I'm not sure whether these are suggestions or reproaches, as Sandro looks clearly experienced in his job.

It has now been a few minutes and Gaetano has not left the kitchen yet, when suddenly I could hear deafening sounds of smashed plates, as well as some loud blasphemies. Chatter stops at the guests' table for a moment, but after a while everything is back to normal. Gaetano leaves the kitchen after a few seconds staggering, with this white shirt all stained by red sauces, shining colours ranging from red to green.

After grabbing a high-waisted apron from Sandro, looking passive-aggressive, Gaetano seems to be in a good mood regardless, going to Conte's table uninvited, to ensure that everything is going smoothly. The daughter does not seem to *have enjoyed the squid salad, and she says so, but Gaetano does not appreciate this and starts saying something about her not having it tasted it properly and that she was plain wrong, as it was one of the best dishes of the restaurant, with a fake patient attitude.*

*Antonio Conte starts looking annoyed and calls Sandro to the table, where they exchange a few whispered words. According to what I can make out of Sandro's looks, he is rather annoyed, so he calls Gaetano over and, looking calm, I see them coming toward my table: I am close enough to hear Sandro say: "You either try to be serious, or this is not on. I asked you for a favour and you are ruining the guests' night. Be careful as this is the last warning I give you". Gaetano pretends to look like he cares and, looking all proper, he starts doing other less important tasks, such as opening bottles of wine and changing cutlery after each course, leaving the rest to the other waiter.*

*Between the first and the second course, the situation seems to improve, and Gaetano seems to be okay in his new role, even if he is increasingly looking bored, frustrated, and tired. While bringing over the fish dish to the table, however, it was clear that the other waiter was struggling to serve the sea bass, due to the scorching hot plates, and he seemed like he was begging Gaetano to go help him. Approaching the struggling colleague to help, Gaetano gets distracted by Antonio Conte's hair, perhaps to see whether the rumours about a wig were true.*

*This distraction makes Gaetano grab a hot dish carelessly, making it fall onto the naked back of Conte's wife, who was celebrating her birthday.*

*I am able to catch the right exact moment where the woman realises what had just happened: honestly, I felt her pain. The scream due to her physical suffering makes everyone jump, as well as Gaetano, who runs to grab some ice in order to fix the situation. However, the ice he was able to get from the wine ice bucket was already half-melted, and his effort to put it onto the woman's back were not well-received.*

*I cannot believe my eyes.*

*Due to the commotion, Conte gets up and starts walking towards poor Gaetano – looking extremely angered - but, noticing him, Gaetano stops trying to fix the situation on the wife's back, and tries to block him by putting his hands in front of himself saying that it was an accident. Slaps and punches start flowing, and Gaetano was not hit by any of that out of pure luck, when all of a sudden, a guest stops Conte from behind, trying to calm him down and trying to defend Gaetano.*

*"I AM TELLING YOU; I WILL GET YOU FIRED TONIGHT, I AM SICK OF YOU". In the meantime, Conte's daughter starts crying for the overall uproar and her screams are confused with the painful cries of the mother, as well as the father's threats. I see Sandro intervene, grabbing Gaetano from his shirt's neck and bringing him downstairs. I get up and follow them].*

6

¤ You are going to stay here now and clean all of these dishes. If in twenty minutes, when I'm back, there is even a single glass still dirty, or a dish with some food on, I will do my best to kick out of here and get you banned from anywhere in London, and from the whole of the United Kingdom. Do you understand?

- It was an accident, it slipped from my hands!

¤ I don't care; you did nothing right. Nothing at all.

Pray to God that what happened tonight will not give the restaurant a bad name, because should it be the case, I'm going to kill you with my bare hands. No jokes.

*[Sandro walks back towards the main room annoyed, trying to manage the situation].*

- Welcome to my life, Marco.

According to a Migrantes report, the United Kingdom is still the preferred destination for Italian migrants, despite Brexit.

# THE FAIR

1


< Thank you so much for coming! I was not expecting it, to be fair: it is not exactly an event attended by people outside of this field of work.
- **No worries, Lorenzo, it is my pleasure.**
< Great, then. Let us go inside, it is freezing out here.
[*We enter the building in front of which we met up, a big warehouse-looking structure off Brick Lane, which is holding a fair for individuals interested in working in the digital sector*].
< I was expecting a bigger hall, to be honest. Oh, well.
I saw the morning's schedule and there are a couple of pitches I am interested in listening to, but apart from that I plan on meeting new people and networking, just to see if I can join any upcoming project. But first, coffee?
- **Sounds amazing to me.**
< That is the way I like it.
What is up with Gaetano? He messaged me last night saying something messy happened but did not explain what exactly.
- **I was with him when he was working. I stayed there at the place all night until closing and Antonio Conte was there, you know, the football manager. He was a guest of the restaurant and he got mad at Gaetano once he dropped some scorching fish on Conte's poor wife's back.**
< No, are you serious? That is hilarious! [*He bursts out laughing*].

- Yes, such a tragic scene. He managed to mess up every single thing. It would be easier to list what he did *not* mess up. They had to literally lift him up and hide him in the backroom washing dishes, otherwise Conte would have actually hit him. Then, when Conte left with all of his guests, they made him clean up the dining room, by himself. To punish him. Poor lad.

< It is incredible. I am not even sure how, but week after week, something weird happens to him…

Coffee is on me, how do you want it? Such a variety of choice, as you can see [*the café – the only one in the massive room – was only listing "coffee" and "English Breakfast tea" in the hot drinks' section*].

Can we have two coffees to take away please? Thank you [*he asks the lady behind the counter*].

Do you want to see something crazy? [*He asks me while he reveals the iWatch on his wrist, placing it on the counter's card reading machine and thanking the barista*]. I have just paid for these two coffees using my watch. I just find it so cool; it is insane. [*We place the hot drinks on a small table in front of the café, where other people did the same*].

When this summer I tried to do the same in a supermarket in Lucca, two old ladies were queuing behind me and as soon as they saw what I did, they must have thought I was a wizard. So funny.

Here in London, I have never really used cash, I never brought any with me either, as cards are accepted everywhere, even in the smallest of off-licences. Every time I go back home, however, it is always so hard to pay by card.

□ Wow, who would have thought that Italians would be here, too! What a coincidence! [*Lorenzo gets interrupted by a guy who was sipping on his coffee on our same table*]. Nice to meet you, I'm Fabio.

< It is the first thing every Italian thinks as soon as they find another Italian around the corner, here in London. Nice to meet you, I am Lorenzo. And he is Marco.

☐ Well said! What brings you here, then?

< Life! [*They both start laughing, more out of embarrassment than fun*].

No, really, jokes aside. I am here because I'd like to change jobs and I feel like meeting new people, you know.

☐ Yes, I definitely feel you! What do you do?

< Well, I do sales in an e-commerce start-up, you?

☐ Interesting! I'm the CEO of a start-up trading Bitcoin…

< Wow, really? [*He starts looking around, seemingly no longer interested in the conversation*].

Look, Marco, they are starting one of those presentations you told me earlier you are interested in over there, shall we go? Pleasure to meet you, Fabio. Good luck for everything!

[*He grabs my right side and starts dragging me away from the table*].

Quick, quick, let us get away from that one as soon as possible. I would have liked to keep chatting to him but unfortunately nothing he said is true. Have they ever told you that story of that twenty-two-year-old Spanish guy who invested fifty euros into Bitcoin five years ago?

**- No, how did that one end?**

< Well, the guy is now twenty-seven.

This shows you why you should be wary of things like that, as they fail in the ninety-five percent of cases, making your hard-earned money disappear into a black hole.

Excuse my rush but I just had to do it. You know, I keep reading LinkedIn posts by people blowing their own trumpet, writing about their successful businesses, when at the end of the day they do not do anything, it is just words on words. Meaningless stuff. I just get so angry, though. The only thing I want to do every time I see a post like that is to write below "GO FUCK YOURSELF!" and go straight to the point.

Like those who write stuff like "Yesterday I attended the most important interview of my life. They asked me "Where do you see yourself in five years?" and I said, 'Doing your job'. The interviewer, emotional, hugs me and gives me a big squeeze. Today I got promoted to CEO". A comment such as "FUCK OFF AND DIE" would have been perfect in this case, what do you reckon?

But then again, shall we talk about those people who ask you "Where do you see yourself in five years"? I must have had at least three interviews, and this is question they always as you last! Once I even answered, "I think I will be dead", highlighting how life is unpredictable and that each action a human being does, at the end of the day it is very hard to have any say in what happens.

Obviously, they never called me back in for a second interview, but I have to admit that was a tiny satisfaction for me, after having so many mean-spirited experiences.

At the end of the day, I learnt that working in London means that you do not get to decide what you will be when you grow up, you simply pick your next slave owner. And in such a dire situation, I need to make sure that I pick the best slave owner I can, right? Given the fact that over here I actually have a chance, a "privilege" that is not always true back home in Italy. Have you ever read Theodore Kaczynski's manifesto? Back in the day he was known as *Unabomber*. If we ignore for a moment the terror attacks he carried out – which I of course condemn and consider nothing else but a senseless and exaggerated effort to show himself off – if you ever get to read his words, you will notice that he uses rather woke words to describe today society, despite writing the book more than twenty years ago now.

What he would have wanted was a society without any technology because, since humans have been living within a continuous industrial revolution, the world has experienced a number of catastrophic consequences, throwing the overall society into depression, stress, and an incredible decline of the human experience by flattening it, and demeaning it innovation after innovation. A specific paragraph has been stuck into my head ever since: when Kaczynski describes human stimuli, meaning those things what encourage humankind to reach a goal. Essentially, he divides these human urges into three groups: those that can be satisfied with minimum effort, those which can be satisfied but only after a massive effort, and those that cannot be satisfied adequately, regardless of how much effort you put in.

Now, I am not in a position to explain to you how and why it happened, but after the industrial revolution, humans have increasingly found themselves in the third group, due to no fault of their own. This is due to the social and economic situation they are experiencing. From blue to white collar people, from young businessmen to young unemployed, consumed by an alienating and mortifying condition.

While reading this booklet, I realised that my frustration was due to the fact that in that time, I was unconsciously belonging in the third group, meaning that I kept sending out CVs to find a job without any actual result or feedback. After re-directing my focus and re-evaluating my essence, I unexpectedly ended up fitting into the second group, as explained earlier. You can call it luck, yeah. I now understand that I could have the chance to get to the first category, to exploit the first urge, and I think it is fair for me to exploit it fully.

This is nothing but a game for me, now. A cruel game where the winner is whoever has the most technical skills and ends up being the most aggressive. A soul-emptying game, replaced by those very skills where everything is a struggle, and not solidarity. I have been a victim of this game for too long now, but now that I understand the rules fully, I am no longer an easy target.

**- But is this not the same exact mechanism that would make you absorb and represent all that mean-spiritedness which is filling all the environments you hate so much?**

< Yes, sure. But I am aware of it. What I am doing is suicide. Or rather, the more I advance, the more I feel my brain shrinking, a bit as if my personality and essence at the end of the day were meaningless. But what kind of worth could a personality have, considering that it is the fruit of homologation, battling with a homologated environment? Nothing whatsoever. I am nothing but a number. A nicely decorated number, a number adorned by tiny little flowers I have been picking over my rather short life so far. But why should other people care? That is why I often think that when all is said and done, it would not be so bad to wear that very mask on my face, just to ensure that I can reach my goals without losing out completely. I know I have been waiting for far too long now and putting it all off, but it is especially because I am not sure whether my mind could take all this in.

**- Are you not fearing change? To perhaps find a worse environment than the one you are leaving?**

< Not at all, no. I think that at this point, if I stay strong, I can change the rules of the game from the inside. I am becoming quite ambitious, you know. I would like to become the chief of some organisation, but in order to succeed, I have to enter an even more exclusive context, and to do so, my identity needs to be much more defined, so that it would become easier for me to mould it according to what I need it to be. The company I am working for at the moment has already reached its peak, so there is not much for me to look forward to. And to be clear – also because we are almost there – all those heads will fall like dominoes very soon.

Anyway, no more chitchat, I think I will be going around for a bit, looking for someone I can suck up to. Feel free to do anything you want. Shall we meet here in a bit, okay?

- **To be fair, I am here to watch what you do…**

< Well, my friend, not now. This is a delicate job; I need to be on my own. Watch other people, come on. Alright? Cool, see you later my friend [*he starts walking decidedly toward another room*].

2


[*I am rather taken aback by Lorenzo's behaviour, but after a while I make peace with it. Although I try to follow him at first, I lose sight of him after many more people in quite tacky suit and tie outfits enter the massive fair.*

*I spend a few minutes watching a presentation about a subscription service which allows customers to join a large number of affiliated gyms all over the United Kingdom. It is defined as the "Netflix of gyms". The guy presenting the project is the typical jacked gym-goer, who tries to explain how everything works by waving his arms around constantly. The language employed in the pitch is full of unnecessary adjectives used to emphasise how innovative and cutting-edge the project is, and motivational quotes on a big screen to show how the right mindset was the key for him to start this business from the grounds up. After reading the sentences "If you can dream it, you can do it", by Walt Disney, I get up and leave.*

*Around the rooms of the conference centre, I notice many stalls and tents with people representing small businesses, trying to grab young aspiring professionals to recruit. In many of these I notice endless queues of hopeful young people holding their CVs in their hands. The bigger the stall, the longer the queue. Some of these also had small, reserved areas next to them, made up of plastic tables full of untouched drinks and finger* food, next to greasy hand-made notes. Everything seemed abandoned, waiting for the cleaning staff to clean up, so that other people would have the chance to use the table the same way as before.

After a while, I notice that rather than networking, these young professionals spend their time on improvised chairs to work on their laptops or to make short phone calls. Many of them seem rather nervous, but others seem completely at ease with the situation, with big smiles on their faces.

I am no longer able to find Lorenzo. The rooms get even more crowded, I finally realise that I do not really belong there, and I start walking toward the exit door, noticing how the rubbish stacked away in less crowded corners has now integrated with the room.

I leave the fair, I message Lorenzo, but he does not even visualise it].

Taking into account both AIRE and non-AIRE registered citizens, almost half a million Italians were living in London in 2017: the same number of people living in Genoa.

# THE CONCERT

1


~ Hello, we are here! Have you been waiting for long?

**- No worries. To be fair I took such a long time to find this place,
I thought it was a pub...**

~ It is a pub. But it is also a concert hall. More of a hall than a
pub to be fair [*she laughs*].

Well, you told me you wanted to meet up in a pub, I did not
disappoint you in the end, right? We can also make the most of
it and enjoy the gig tonight. A cool group is playing, they are a
bit like the early days of Tame Impala, they are called The
Holydrug Couple.

Welcome to Shacklewell Arms, my absolute favourite place in
London. I have seen so many cool groups here...

[*Serena and I enter the place*].

~ From Mystic Braves to Scott Yoder, from Bee Bee Sea to King
Khan and BBQ Show...What do you know of these people,
though. The very first gigs by Idles in London, by King Gizzard
and The Lizard Wizard and by Fat White Family, they were all
here! It is not a simple pub; it is an actual place of worship.

Anyway, the gig is in around an hour, fancy a pint?

Thanks for coming, I can't be bothered being alone at a gig. I
like having someone to comment on how they play, also
because when I do it on my own on Twitter, people around me
look at me weirdly.

Lol, it was so easy with you, you really thought it would be just
a quick drink with me... Cute.

[*We grab the beers, and we sit down*].

~ You know what I really love about this city? Apart from how amazing the music is at concerts – even in the smallest of locations, and trust me, I have been to so many gigs since I have been here. Anyhow, the best thing is that concerts end at around ten or eleven o'clock, at the latest. It gives me so much peace. In Italy, hours like these are unthinkable, so many times shows do not even start till eleven.

By the way, cheers!

What was I telling you just now? Ah, yes. This is my safe place, also because I based my life on selecting the best music only, and each person who enters from that front door, in my opinion, deserves to be met. Also, because, and keep this in mind, musical selection is the new natural selection.

The outside world is cruel, full of people with Instagram pages full of selfies and who still listen to the same music they enjoyed ten years ago. You know those people who like, say, twenty of your pictures, but then do not follow you back? Yeah, I am talking about that kind of people, a bit like those friends you want to go see stuff with, and then they ghost you. Bastards.

This world only wants attention without giving anything back: a coping mechanism is to self-isolate not to be annoyed, even though often this very world comes back to bite you, exactly because you force yourself to isolate. And this is because there should be more places like the Shacklewell Arms: it is a good excuse to refuse others' absurd demands, from brunching, to some overpriced coffee date in an anonymous Starbucks café, *poffarbacco*[20].

Why have people stopped saying *poffarbacco*? It is such an amazing word; I personally would always use it. *Poffarbacco.*

Anyway, have you heard about what happened to Gaetano? It was so funny…

---

[20] Italian expression for "Goodness gracious".

Gaetano is great. He cracks me up every single time. Look, even if he were to hit me in the middle of the road or break my legs with some massive metal bar or smash my phone on my forehead and steal my bag, I would still think highly of him. [*She sips her pint slowly*].

**- Have you got anything else to say about your story? Last time we met up you only told me a few things... We only spoke about Gaetano.**

~ Nah, that's not true, I told you what I had to say. What else can I say? I do not think you care about the fact that when I was sixteen, I had a YouTube channel where I sang nursery rhymes with a metal twist. So funny, with "*La Bella Lavanderina*"[21]. I think the videos had around three hundred thousand views. So many parents left comments under my video saying that I am sick in the head, as my songs scared their kids. Good times. Another thing I can tell you is that I used to have a very well-curated Tumblr account, which I updated every day.

You know, I started programming thanks to this: I was so annoyed when all the available themes were a bit meh, so I went deeper and started messing with the HTML, modifying them all. They were amazing and I did it all by myself. Since all these Boomers' arrival on Facebook – around a couple of years ago or so – I kept using Tumblr and I became better and better at programming.

So annoying, since Instagram has come around and become popular, it has also become way less interesting. Good things are always short-lived, *poffarbacco*.

**- Then, why are you not working as a programmer, but instead work at Primark?**

~ Well, you know, this is an option I keep considering, but at the end of the day I decided that programming needs to remain just a passion of mine. I do not want to get to the point where

---

[21] Italian's children street song, meaning "The Pretty Cleaner".

I get to hate it: I have seen so many of my *mutuals* who made a job out of their passion and the majority of them now hates what they do.

Besides, a few months ago Lorenzo, Gaetano's friend, suggested we should try and create a new platform to help bands to find available places where to perform, and to help club owners and such to find new bands to fill their nights. He introduced him to me this summer, I did not think that he was one of those people I would have gone out with often, but his idea seemed really interesting. That is why I told him that I was happy to work with him: we would meet up at Gaetano's shop when we were not at work, and we would sit down together thinking about how to make it.

The thing is that the more we would work on the app, the more Lorenzo wanted to take leads of the whole project, dismissing my own knowledge, when he was not even able to use CTRL-ALT-DELETE. I was trying to embellish the code, but he did not notice how good it was getting, rather the opposite. He kept pushing me to work more and more, giving me random deadlines, and even when I met them, he still was not satisfied with anything. You can't even imagine how many perfectly functioning endpoints he forced me to remake – after days or weeks of work – just because the result was not exactly what he wanted? Then after a while he started being obsessed with this money-making talk, trying to find ways to manage this project, which was not even a thing yet. Mad stuff. I did not even care about any of this, to be honest.

Our relationship turned from a colleague-to-colleague one, to something where I was being treated as a slave, and where my experience and times were not respected whatsoever. So, in the end I told him he could go on by himself if he wanted to, and that if his goal was to work in a start-up, mine was definitely not. To be honest, I felt a bit sorry about all this, as this project was rather close to my heart.

Since then, when Gaetano asks me to go out and he tells me he is coming, I thank him but refuse his invitation. I can't see him; I can't even hear his name. I hate him with all my heart because he made me unconsciously hate what I used to like. It took me weeks to realise that I was not the problem, but he was. In the end, the project was abandoned because he could not find anyone else to work for him, basically unpaid.

Oh well, let's talk about something else now. I get annoyed just thinking about it.

The place is getting fuller, nice! Do you want to know something fun? Just by looking at the people, I can figure out who came here for the gig and who only for a beer. Look at that guy behind you [*I turn and look at this tiny guy – by himself – sitting a couple of tables further back*]. Yeah, he is definitely here for the gig because *shoegaze*, the Holydrug Couple's genre, is definitely for people who find it difficult to ask for something over the counter. And he most certainly has this problem because it has now been fifteen minutes and he had no luck getting the attention of either the waitress or the barman. I see him raising his arm every time someone who works here walks by him, poor man. So funny.

Do you know what I would not mind doing when I grow up? Suggesting music to people. It only takes me ten minutes after speaking to someone, to understand what his general vibe is, and I guess correctly what their favourite music is.

It is definitely not a simple thing, yeah. Everyone tells me that I have a gift and that this talent of mine would work much better than all of the various YouTube and Spotify algorithms.

For example, you look like someone who would love The Horrors, The KVB, maybe a bit of Weyes Blood as well.

**- Who?**

~ Yeah, there you go. You give me that chronic depressing vibe, but one of those people who pretend to be depressed, not sure if you know what I mean. I guess, someone with so many emotions inside [*I nod just to make her continue, even though I have no idea what she is saying*]. I think you will like the group playing tonight. Actually, I am sure of it.

Please, never be someone who listens to four records a year – normally artists with millions of fans – and complains about current music, about the fact that "nothing interesting gets released anymore, and that once upon a time, things were better". You'd better not be, because I would strangle all of those people who think like that.

- **No, I am rather open-minded** [*I reply, a bit scared*].

~ Okay, I believe you.

I am just saying because I know that type of people very well, those people who do not take any interest in learning more about small new bands, both Italian and foreign. They prefer to remain in their comfort zone of the past, in their warm and cosy nests, thinking about this nostalgia that really should not even exist. That nostalgia stops their curiosity, and without being curious, their life experiences will be limited, and so will their opinions.

And this is the very reason why in these environments, another type of people I hate come into being: those who say that girl bands suck. Yeah, here misogyny meets hatred: most of them say so without even having listened to a female artist, I am sure of it.

In so many musical genres, female voices can be exceptional at times. To be more precise, I think that within the indie-folk genre, they are ten times better than their male counterparts. But also, in dream-pop and synth-pop. I would give you some examples, but I am sure you would not understand the references [*I nod embarrassed, still frightened by those very strong stances*].

These people are the reason why concerts are happening less and less in Italy. They never go to one. Clubs and concert halls are always half empty when less known but talented artists play.

This group here, The Holydrug Couple, would have never played in Italy, and I would have never got to know them. And this makes me so angry, *ghe sboro*[22].

I am not saying that Italians do not like music, but it is a fact that not all of them want to listen to an unknown band, whereas here people are much more open-minded in this sense. It is a pity, because there are so many talented bands in Italy from both melodic and sound points of view, I mean, we are not all rubbish. Could there be more? Absolutely. But in these conditions, an artist is simply not motivated to become a musician. So many times, people make fun of them for the simple fact that they are artists. Imagine girls who want to follow this path, impossible!

Unfortunately, people prefer crappy music, and they go crazy for those con artists who publish some tracks on Spotify, get a high number of streams and disappear into a black hole. I see them as proper scumbags because it is known that some of them buy all the streams just to be called up to be asked to perform.

At the end of the day, each to their own, but I really can't understand this intellectual poverty.

[*She finishes drinking her beer*].

Okay, do you mind going to stand the front of the parterre? The gig should start any minute now.

[*We start walking toward the room next to the one we were drinking in*].


2


~ I am excited, I can't wait for the gig to start [*she looks around to see the people in the room*].

---

[22] Vulgar Italian expression from the region of Veneto, signifying that you have strong feelings about something.

You see, another interesting thing about London is that audiences, in general, are quite varied. I mean that, if you focus, it is a mix between middle-aged and younger people. Something which does not happen in Italy, or better, not around where I am from. In Italy, there is no such thing as seeing gigs in small clubs and such, to be honest it is quite rare to see places allowing up and coming artists to perform. And when you go to some of their concerts, everyone there is really young.

I like seeing grey hair here and there, it makes me realise that even when we get older, the love for music remains. Also, because I just can't imagine a life without gigs if I am honest.

**- Are you afraid of getting older?**

~ Well, who is not? In my case, everyone who got older also got bitchier.

I really would not want to end up like that.

Thinking of adult age, I think of that stuff, to be fair. A time of your life when all you do is work and hang out with people chatting about work. Everything else is seen as unnecessary, what kind of life is that?

And when I think about it, sometimes I wish I could isolate myself even more and boost my passions. I would do anything not to become like them, like Lorenzo, for instance.

That kind of massive ego fuelled by your professional role – and not by who you are – is the worst disgrace that hit humankind in the last century.

This constant urge to find a place in this world, talking about "the future", convinced that you can change it somehow: I hate all this. Thinking about the future is such an abstract and imprecise concept, detached from the present moment. Rather, thinking about our own personal strengths objectively is the right step to reach our goals, or at least this is what I believe. And this is what our generation is missing. Or, better, in my opinion we are getting there, but the selfishness of the everyday businessman is still way too strong.

I honestly think that all this awareness I have is due to all those books I have been reading throughout my teenage years. First of all, Orwell, and Huxley, damn it. Therefore, take everything I say with a grain of salt.

I could have become like everyone else, taking selfies with my friends from our towns at our usual dinner party. With those huge grins on their faces. I could have perhaps remained in Treviso, kept in touch with my old childhood friends, avoided challenging myself this way and left things untouched. I could have also become one of those people who show off money they do not have, going to posh places just to fill their Instagram profiles of pictures only to make their friends jealous. And instead… The more I watch some people's stories, the more I notice that they are not really having fun, but they only portray an image of fictional fun.

At times, I tell myself how easier and more carefree my life would have been if I had been like that. Then I think about it and the first thing I feel is discomfort, which turns into disgust. I reject all this whenever I think about it.

You know, every now and then I have a few moments – between some Netflix series and the other – where I see my reflection on the black screen of my laptop, and I ask myself what I am doing with my life. But then I keep telling myself that I am doing exactly what I enjoy, and all my worries disappear.

I am here to go to shows where lesser-known bands play and make me feel good, and London is full of concerts that ignite my curiosity and willingness to discover new things day by day. I can't see myself outside of this environment.

*[The lights in the room go out, and people stop chatting. The Holydrug Couple's drummer and the guitarist – and singer – make their entrance on stage and the parterre starts shouting*

*excitedly, clapping loudly alongside it. Serena jumps on the spot, happy].*

3

*[Once the loudness dies down, the band starts playing. Between echoes and undulating sounds, the audience listens to the group attentively. Some move following the rhythm, others take their phones out of their pockets and start recording excitedly.*
*Serena is mesmerised by what is happening on stage: looking at the drums, she makes me notice how good the drummer is, thanks to his precise touches and, at times, muffled. The singer and guitarist fine-tunes his voice to make it sound like a hypnotic echo. Serena whispers into my year that without those adjustments, his voice would be hardly enjoyable due to various dissonances, but she quickly adds that it is common in that genre – the neo-psychedelic – as they all have the same issue and therefore, they prefer to improve their style by adding a few tricks. The guitar, on the other hand, is played using non-trivial chords, closely following the hits of the drums. All of this set of details creates a jumble of melodic sounds, as well as rather enchanting, vaguely recalling the psychedelic sounds of the 60s and 70s. There are also a few moments when Serena points to the beauty of the drummer, but she spends most of the night swaying in the crowd.*
*The environment created was so intimate, and all of my perceptions were heightened, mainly thanks to the sound quality from the room's speakers and amplifier. Serena was definitely right about that. I start enjoying the gig, and I start moving my body to the music, too. I am actually loving that: I feel it loud and clear in my bones and I end up shivering after a solo – always reverberated - which felt endless, even though*

*it only lasted a few minutes. Serena was right about something else, too: I really like this band]*.

According to a recent survey, around 80% of Italian citizens living (or who have lived) in the United Kingdom, are happy with their choice.

# DOGE

1


- They fired me, *compà*. After over a year working for them. And for what? Because the bossy customer complained to the boss after such a tiny lapse.

And I can't do anything because I was not working legally, can you believe this? I mean, look, I'm shocked. They also added that another reason why they took this decision was that often I missed work, but this is just a massive lie. I always went to work, never skipped a single day, it was definitely wrong for them to tell me such thing.

Ah, what can I do now, the damage is already done. I can't do anything about this anymore.

You know what I learnt from this experience? That society forces you to be excellent all the time, therefore if you suck at something, that becomes a moral duty.

- **Very well said, Gaetano, did you make that up?**

- Yes, I read it on Facebook the other day.

- **What will you do now?**

- Well, a couple of days ago I heard someone I know saying that in his company, based in Peckham, are always looking for staff. They do door-to-door sales, and apparently, they earn a very good wage.

I'm going to meet him very soon, by the way, he invited me to some event where he will present something.

So, are you coming along? No, wait, I'm making you come. No excuses.

Listen, shall we eat something? I'm starving…

- **Sounds good.**

[*We enter an Italian deli in Soho*].

- Look Marco, so much good food in here.

Every time I come here it makes me want to cry.

[*He points at the products for me*].

They have Gocciole[23], Estathè[24], Italian cream. All those things that British people don't have, poor them.

My God, they also have chickpeas! See, these are real chickpeas, look at them [*he shoves a tin of chickpeas by a famous Italian brand into my face*]. Do you know why I'm saying this? Because the best part of chickpeas aren't chickpeas themselves, but their water. And only Italian chickpeas have the best aquafaba, trust me. English chickpeas are so disgusting, a kick in the guts for who loves chickpeas like me.

Compared to my own deli, this place looks like a food hall. I feel so at peace right now [*he keeps scouring attentively each and every product on the shelves*].

They also have Paneangeli[25], pandoro, buffalo mozzarella. My God. I don't want to leave this place! Pinch me, am I dreaming? Amaretti, Marco, they also have amaretti!

These almond sweets are typical of my area. And, indeed, look here [*he points to the label*], "Made in Guarcino, Frosinone". I'm so moved, really [*he sniffs*]. I'd buy everything if I only could.

[*A girl behind the counter tries to approach us*].

∴ Hi there, do you need anything in particular?

- Hi, are you Italian? [*Gaetano asks the shop assistant while looking at the products in the shop's window, excited*].

---

[23] Very popular biscuits made of shortcrust pastry and chocolate chips.

[24] Lemon and/or peach tea, made by Ferrero. Like Gocciole, they too are very popular in Italy.

[25] Italian brand specialised in baking powder and yeast, used to prepare pizza and focaccia.

∴ No, I'm Polish.
- Ah, alright [*he looks at her annoyed, as if not being Italian were her fault*].
How is this sandwich?
∴ Tuna, tomato and mayo, dear.
- Mmh, alright, a large cup of barley coffee, then. And a cream croissant. Are you eating?
- **No, thanks. I am not hungry.**
- Cool. Sweetheart, can we sit?
∴ Yes, no worries. I will bring you everything.
- Thanks [*we sit at a table*].
Jesus Christ, these Polish are everywhere, man. We're all either Italian or Spanish or Polish in London, I'm sick of this. It's so hard to meet English people here, let alone Londoners [*he lowers his voice*].
Anyways, Martina hasn't replied to my texts for days. I don't know what to do with these women, honestly.
- **Why, has something happened?**
- No, I'm really not sure what could have happened. Look [*he shows me his phone, pointing at the blue ticks on WhatsApp*]. I have been messaging her for two days now, but it is only blue ticks, not even a reply.
- **To be honest with you yeah, it is a bit worrying.**
- Lorenzo told me that she has been in her room all day every day because she has been writing an essay, however a phone call every once in a while can't be that much of an effort [*he sighs*].
- **Has Lorenzo added anything else?**
- No. He told me you went to that fair together, but he did not speak about Martina. Now that I think about it, he always tries to change the subject when I ask him about her.
[*The lady brings what we ordered to the table while looking at Gaetano sideways*]. Thank you, thanks a million.

What the fuck are you looking at, mug [*he whispers to himself as soon as the girl turns her back*].
∴ Have you said anything?
- No, thank you again, pretty [*he smiles awkwardly*].
[*Gaetano dips his croissant in his drink and bites it while it is still dripping*].
Such good pastry, mate.
It is so annoying though, Jesus Christ. This work thing was the last thing I needed. As if I had no problems already.
I'm late on my rent, a week or so I think. If they don't pay me for the last month, they will probably kick me out of the house. I also wanted to get those shoes with little wheels below the sole. You know which ones I mean, the ones that kids like? Well, they make them for adults as well. It would save me so much time. But I can't do that now, damn it.
- **Lorenzo is looking for a new job as well, maybe he can help you out and tell you where to look.**
- No way, whatever he does is not for me whatsoever. Don't worry, I will find a solution anyway.
- **Okay, I was just looking to help you.**
- Yeah, exactly. I know what to do.
[*He finishes his croissant and his drink, he gets up and pays the bill, he thanks the lady again and we walk toward the exit*].


2


[*Once at the event, after a few minutes, we decided to give it a go. Inside, we see around fifteen people who occupied a quarter of the seats, and the only person in a suit and tie was the host, Gaetano's friend.*
*What we notice at first is an eerie silence, nobody in the audience was speaking to anyone. Other things which stood out were massive signs hung on every wall stating DOGE, which is the name of the company, in WordArt style. There was also a*

*fifteen-inch laptop for the presentation and two large coffee containers, for the audience to drink once the event was over. The host does not waste time and after greeting us, he invites us to sit down as the presentation would have started in a few moments. I use this time to look around the room and I notice the confused and lost look on the attendees: still, with no expression. You could tell they were embarrassed].*

♠ Welcome everyone! Thanks for being here, there are so many of you! I wish I could hug you all right now because it is only thanks to you that we are succeeding in getting more and Italian Londoners involved. Indeed, I see so many few faces here! [*He looks in our direction*].

Big applause for our new arrivals! [*A lazy applause welcomes us, Gaetano seems pleased*].

Well, I want to have the veterans say a few words about who we really are, as our company is not made by our products, it is made by our personalities and by who we really are. Paolo, would you like to tell us something about yourself?

[*A middle-aged man stands up and starts speaking*].

♣ Hello everyone, my name is Paolo and after I started using DOGE's products, my life has changed. I lost twenty-four kilos in a year by drinking two cups of tea every day [*Another applause*].

I also had Type 2 diabetes. Doctors told me I had only three or four years to live if I had not stopped eating what I was eating and had not stopped with my unhealthy lifestyle. They told me I had to enjoy life while it lasted, spending time with loved ones. However, just five days ago I got the best news ever: thanks to my weight loss, doctors told me my diabetes is getting better and that I can go back to living my life in all freedom [*Another applause started*].

Ladies and gentlemen, DOGE's infusions and meal replacements are really miraculous. Two weeks ago, this nice lad here [*he grabs the arm of a sixteen or seventeen-year-old boy sitting next to him]* got a nasty rash on his left arm. We went to every dermatologist in the city, they prescribed some medicine, but nothing worked.

One day, almost by chance, I suggested he should start drinking DOGE's chamomile each night.

Michele, show everyone how your arm is now [*the boy lifts his sweater's sleeve, showing the full arm and showing no sign of eczema. Gaetano looks the most surprised in the audience and yet another applause starts*].

♠ Thank you, thank you Paolo and Michele.

A true story, ladies and gentlemen. This is what happens to people who drink DOGE beverages regularly. Wellness. Are you still not entirely convinced yet? Roberta, do you want to say anything?

[*The host passes the microphone to a tiny lady, sitting in the front row*].

♦ Thank you so much. I regularly drink DOGE instant decaffeinated coffee and have been doing so for the past three years. I can tell you honestly that I have survived colon cancer thanks to this incredible brew.

Doctors were not able to explain how the hell I managed to survive cancer without chemotherapy, they told me I was done. They saw me as the walking dead. But oh well, here I am! I thank the good Lord for the miracle he did. I am here to say that DOGE products work, and I am a living proof of it. [*Another applause started, and this time Gaetano managed to do a standing ovation*].

[*The host asks other two guests to speak, this time they are a bit older and less convincing. One of them claims that DOGE coffee improved their life for the better, and the other one swore that his gut health, which has been compromised for many years, was perfect now. The same agenda all the time: DOGE's products were miraculous and were much better than traditional drugs.*]

*The presenter managed to catch many people's attention thanks to those examples and testimonials, but Gaetano was especially and totally mesmerised by the astounding results that people claimed to have experienced.*
*At the end of the presentation, some sort of auction house had been created, where people who bought three or more boxes would have got a discount. Gaetano buys four and – when everyone left the room – he stays to chat with the friend].*

3


**- What did you talk about?**
- I got the job! Jesus, I'm so happy! Look here [*he uses his chin to point to the boxes he had with him*], he gave me a discount and he told me that all I had to do now was to sell them.
I need to be quick to do it as time flies and time is money! By the way, do you want anything? Some chamomile tea, or coffee? The price is more than fair.
**- No Gaetano, I am fine. Also, because I am about to leave London and would not know how to bring them home as I am flying.**
- No, fair enough. Come on, I can send them to you though, if you want!
Okay, you know what? I'm going to call all the friends I have here, I'm sure I can find someone who is interested in buying these [*he takes his phone out, asks me to hold the boxes, and calls Serena*].
Serè? Hey!

...

Were you sleeping?

...

Oh, you are off today.

...

Sorry, my fault.

Listen, I have something for you.

…

It's a surprise!
Are you free in half an hour?
I'm not too far from your flat, I can come by.

…

Cool, nice one. Let's go!
Give me your postcode and I'm coming to you.

…

Yes, yes, Marco is here too.
Cool, cool. See you in a bit!
Bye, bye.
[*He hangs up the phone, takes the boxes back and gives me a nod, to say that I should follow him outside. We start walking towards the exit*].
Done and dusted, Serena will be my first customer. She said we can go to her place. She lives in New Cross, not too far from here, just a few Overground stops. I can't wait…
- **Does she know you are going around to sell this stuff?**
- No, I told her that it's a surprise, precisely [*he winks at me*].
It is the first time I go to her house; you know. She lives with an old woman and she is doing well for herself. She basically keeps Serena just to have some company – and for some housework, as if she were a slave – in exchange of a rent that's slightly below average. The girl is smart, let me tell you!
[*We walk by a stall with people looking for signatures, one of them intercepts Gaetano*].
√ Hello mate, would you like to sign our petition against drugs? Every year, thousands of people in England…
- Sorry, I can't. Bye [*he starts walking faster*].
Do I really look like someone who would sign a petition against drugs? [*He laughs on his own*].
Those people who really think that they are fixing issues petition after petition make me mad… WOW, HOLD ON A

SECOND. I'VE JUST HAD A GREAT IDEA. [*We stop in front of a block of flats, Gaetano has eyed an abandoned pram. He hands me his heavy boxes once again while he checks how the pram works. As soon as he realizes that it still works somehow, he asks me to place the boxes on it*].

IT WORKS! Sweet Lord, this is the most incredible day of my life. I saved myself so much work.

- **What if it is someone's?**

- Ah, you're so naïve. You must know that here in England, when people want to get rid of something without having to go to the tip, they put it outside of their houses so that if someone comes by and needs it, they can just take it. I find this super smart. You know how many chairs, couches, and tables you can find this way? I got my mattress like this...

[*While we turn the corner toward the Overground station, I look back and where we found the pram, there was now a confused and angry man, holding a toddler in his arms*].

- **There is a man with his daughter who is looking for his pram...**

- Where?

- **Exactly where you found it... I have just seen it.**

- Well, you snooze, you lose, dude! Or better, you lose a pram! [*He laughs*]. Nice one. I'm so fun, man.

According to a study by SWG, more than one Italian in two declares to have a relative, friend or acquaintance currently living in the United Kingdom.

# FOMODOPAMINE

1


- We should be here; Google Maps says it should be that house over there… Maybe I should message her instead.
[*A door behind us opens up*].
~ *Uè tosi*[26], I am here!
[*Serena glances at the pram, looking frightened*].
What is that? Did you have a baby and you did not tell me?
- No [*Gaetano shows the boxes*], I needed the pram to bring the surprise to you here. We found it…
- **…he stole it…**
- …borrowed in Peckham. I've got a new job!
~ Already?! Well done, you! [*Serena hugs him*].
I am so happy! What do you do?
- This! [*He points to the boxes*].
Can I come in? [*We enter the house, leaving the pram at the entrance and bringing the DOGE boxes inside the living room*].
Wow, what a lovely house, look here. You really know what's best, don't you?
Is the old one at home?
~ Charlotte? She is not that old, come on. She is only around sixty. No, she should be home in a while, she went to Waitrose not long ago.
How come?

---

[26] A word used in Venetian dialect, especially in the Eastern part of the region, meaning "guys".

- No reason… Are you home alone, then? [*He slouches on an armchair*]. Being home alone is such a luxury, I have never had the chance to do so since I have been living in London.
~ Well no shit, *amore*, you are always living with four hundred people. I would have found it hard to be home alone as well if I were in your situation…
Anyways, tell me about your new job!
- I came over exactly for this [*he cackles*].
~ So, yeah, what about all these boxes? What is in them?
- The best investment you could ever made, my friend. For your own health.
[*Serena tenses up*].
~ Gaetano, look, I know already where you are going with this…
[*Gaetano gets up, shuts her up by placing a finger on her lips and he makes her sit where he was sitting earlier*].
- Have you ever heard of *fomodopamine*?
~ To be honest, no. Actually, I have heard the words FOMO[27] and dopamine, but just to describe a phenomenon and a chemical substance linked to social media use.
I do not think I have heard the word *fomodopamine*, no.
- I believe you, my friend. It's an extremely new substance, extracted from *woodwardia radicans*, a prehistoric fern that has leaves larger than three meters. It was recently discovered in the Apennine mountains in Calabria. There's no other place in the whole world where you can find it, and Calabrian woods are full of these fantastic plants. Like, full of them.
Some scientists have realised that by pulverising the leaves of this plant they can obtain a substance, the *fomodopamine* – that is – which can solve all of humankind's hardest struggles.
~ What about that depression caused by an incompatibility with the environment in which you were born, which leads you

---

[27] Acronym standing for "Fear of missing out".

to have a perpetual identity crisis which in turns pushes you to run away all the time when, actually, running away does nothing else but worsen your problem, making you even more depressed?
- Not that, no. Sorry.
~ Not interested, then.
Are you sure about the existence of this substance?
- Of course it exists, crazy. Wait, I don't think you get this. There are people who lost over fifty kilos thanks to fomodopamine, who healed after having the worst cancers of the world, and also beat diabetes!
[*Serena grabs her phone and starts googling the name*].
~ No results here…
[*Gaetano ignores her*].
- Do you want to know something else? DOGE – the company I work for – found the way to put this drug inside the majority of things we eat every single day.
[*Gaetano opens one of the four boxes and takes out colourful packages*].
We've got four types of instant coffee, chamomile, tea, infusions… We also sell the super tasty coffee-flavoured soda branded DOGE, with fomodopamine inside [*he takes a can out, opens it and moves it closer to Serena to make her taste it*]. Try it, it's so good…
[*Serena looks at him sideways, but she plays along. She takes the tin and takes a sip*].
~ Mmh… [*she gags*].
No, Gaetano. Take this stuff away from me because I am going to throw up in your face right now. It tastes like carbonated piss, literally.
Bleah, Jesus Christ it is disgusting. I need water, oh my God.
- If you want, we also have DOGE water!

~ No, leave me alone, you can drink that shit yourself. I am going to the kitchen for a second. [*Gaetano grabs the can back, visibly irritated, while Serena goes to the kitchen*].

- How can you say something like this if you haven't even tasted it properly… [*he takes a sip, makes sure he tastes all of it by keeping the liquid in his mouth as if it were mouthwash, and then he swallows it loudly*].

It has an aftertaste of… [*he retches violently*] of…

- **Gaetano?**

- I'm fine, I'm fine. An aftertaste which reminds me of coff… [*he vomits violently and some of it ends up right between the couch and the Persian carpet in the living room, but a few splashes also end up on my shoes as well as on his trainers*]. Gosh, Serena, I'm so sorry.

[*Moaning, he tries to enter the kitchen, but in the meantime, he vomits again rather violently, staining the laminate below him. Trying to walk convulsively forward, he finds himself stepping on his own vomit which makes him slip, causing him to hit his back on the floor. What was whining has now turned into desperation.*]

~ Gaetano, what was that?

[*Serena comes back from the kitchen holding a glass of water and finds Gaetano in front of her, looking poorly with sick all around him*].

GAETANO, WHAT HAPPENED?

- It wasn't my intention, Serena… [*he sobs*].

I didn't think it would be this disgusting… I'm going to help you clean up everything, I promise…

[*The front door unlocks, opens up and the landlord makes her entrance holding two shopping bags in her hands*].

∧ I'm back, love!

[*Charlotte finds herself in front of Serena as she tries to help Gaetano get up with his back covered in his own vomit, and with the precious furniture ruined by massive stains a bit*]

*everywhere, while I am trying to clean my shoes. She starts having a panic attack and she drops the bags].*
What the fuck.

2


*[Screams and thuds come from the kitchen after Charlotte, recovering from the shock, asks Serena to speak privately. In the meantime, I help Gaetano clean up the disaster].*
- What a moron. I'm such a retard. I never do anything right. Wherever I go, something unpleasant always happens. What a dick, what an idiot.
- **Gaetano, come on now, you could not have known that that soda would have made you vomit... Now you know.**
- I really hope you are not going to write about what has just happened in your article.
- **No, of course not.**
- Thank Marco, you are a true friend. I'm worried about Serena now; I hope she won't be kicked out.
*[Serena leaves the kitchen slamming the door].*
- Serena, everything okay?
~ Not at all, she told me to leave, this bitch. I need to pick up my things and leave in half an hour. Thanks a million Gaetano and your fucking fomodopaminic products.
*[She goes upstairs stomping her feet and slams her bedroom door].*
- *Eccallà*[28]. Well, I thought they would have got their hands on me... *[In the meantime, the landlord comes out of the kitchen].*
- Miss Charlotte, I'm so sorry...
∧ Get out of my house. Now.
*[We leave with no objections, scared of her decisiveness. While Gaetano tries to apologise once more to Charlotte, he picks up*

---

[28] "There it is" in English, this is a Roman interjection that someone says when something predictable happens, mostly an unlucky event.

*DOGE's boxes to put them back on the pram and, telling me to take it, he signals that we should wait for Serena outside the house, twenty meters or so away].*

- **What is your plan now, then?**

- Well, wait and see…

*[Serena leaves the house after a few minutes, with her there are two small suitcases. Gaetano intercepts her].*

- Serena, listen to me, I'm sorry about what happened…

~ I am sorry, too. Sorry for yelling at you, it was not my intention, it was a bit of an overreaction from my part. Charlotte and I have not really been getting along for the past two months and this was the last straw…

- I…

~ No worries, Gaetano, it was not your fault. Do not worry about it.

- Thanks for understanding. Where are you staying now?

~ Well, that is a good question.

- Come stay at my place. You can stay in my room. I'll ask Martina if she can put me up for a few days, until you find somewhere else.

~ Are you sure? I think I remember that she is not really allowed to do stuff like that…

- Yes, totally. I'll win her over this time.

~ Look, I do not want to be a burden…

- If you're in this situation, it's my fault and I need to fix this somehow. It is literally the least I could do.

~ Okay, then.

*[We walk toward the Overground].*

- Guys, do you know that the part behind the knee is called popliteal fossa? I didn't, I've just found out.

3

*[Once at Wood Green, after showing Serena his house and bedroom, and after having spoken to his flatmates to see whether they were okay with the arrangement, Gaetano leaves the house with a backpack and once again grabs the pram with the four boxes on].*
- I spoke to Serena…
- **About?**
- About the fact that Martina hasn't returned any of my texts or calls in days.
- **I thought about your situation and…**
- No, I don't give a shit about this stuff now. I need to understand if Martina is holding a grudge because of me or because something happened, or not. And I need to understand this right now, otherwise I have no place to stay tonight.
- **So?**
- So, I called Lorenzo up and I asked him to meet as soon as he finishes work. His office is near Liverpool Street, we are going to meet him now.
- **Does he know that you are going there to ask him to stay at his place?**
- No.
- **Cool. Great, then…**
- You really are a crappy journalist: you try to keep this posh attitude by not speaking and by not showing emotions, but I never heard you ask a smart question…
- **I am not a journalist yet, Gaetano… How many times do I have to tell you this?**

Scientific studies in clinical settings have demonstrated that there is a very high risk of developing mental disorders for Italians who have decided to move abroad.

# THE GUSTI-BUS

1

- How many times did we use the Underground today?
- **So many...**
- Jesus, no wonder I'm shattered.
[*We stay silent, Gaetano looks at the people around him sleepily, while the tube announcer tells us that we are approaching King's Cross Station*].
- **Is this us?**
- No, we should change at Holborn, it is quicker like that.
- **Okay.**
**Why did you bring the pram with you?**
- Because I just can't leave this stuff at home. I'm sure that I can sell each one of these boxes between today and tomorrow. Besides, I'm not even sure where I would store them, there is not enough room where I live, and I don't trust my flatmates. Yesterday I found this note on the fridge saying, "Next time someone steals my food, I swear I will kill them", signed by the Greek guy living in the bedroom next to mine.
- **Are you afraid that someone is going to steal your instant coffee?**
- No, I'm scared that the Greek guy will burn my boxes once he learns that it was me who ate all of his pork slices.
- **Gaetano...**
- Well, I was hungry... I can't afford to go food shopping since they sacked me. I did not think that he would notice!

- **But you bought those DOGE boxes…**
- Yes, but those are an investment. It is not the same thing.
- **How much did you buy them for?**
[*Gaetano whispers something*].
- **I did not get that…**
- … pounds.
- **Louder, Gaetano!**
- TWO HUNDRED POUNDS.
Okay?!
Stop looking at me like that, I did it to survive… Don't think that I'm a bad person just because I've only got around a hundred pounds in my bank account.
[*The silence on the carriage was interrupted by Gaetano, and the passengers were visibly annoyed, so much that someone tries to shut Gaetano up*].
OH, SHUSH!
[*Gaetano snaps back at the fearless commuter*].
I have felt judged from the first moment I arrived in this city. Nothing that I do is ever right. I ran away from Ceprano because of this, I don't want the same situation to happen here, too. Don't you start now, please!
I have been here for over a year, in a country that is not mine, where everyone speaks a different language, aware that I keep feeling like nothing but a wasteman.
And do you want to know what really pisses me off? That, should I go back home, I would feel the exact same way. With people my age thinking of me as a stranger because I have not been hanging out with them for ages, and they would be right! You know, sometimes I have this feeling, I feel like a dirty immigrant. A nomad who doesn't even know where his home really is anymore. I can't go back now, and the only hope I have left is to keep dreaming about one day having a family of my own, with a house of my own. And now that not even Martina seems to care about me, I'm not sure about what to do…

[*He starts crying*].
- **Gaetano...** [*I apologise for dismissing his feelings, I try to comfort him, but he keeps sobbing loudly*].
- According to Serena, Martina and Lorenzo are together and they are both trying to hide it... [*he tries to put himself together and sniffs*].
- **Why would she think that?**
- She says she just feels it. She said that to me earlier when I was making her bed.
- **I understand.**
**You do not think so?**
- I'm not sure.
- **Serena is not a fan of Lorenzo because of the way he treated her when they were working together. You need to remember that. Maybe she is wrong... Maybe it was just a thoughtless statement.**
- But what if it's not? Normally she is always right. I don't want to think about it, my head hurts.
[*We get off at Holborn station to change for the Central line, towards Liverpool Street. The train arrives quickly, and we jump on it, but we spend the rest of the journey sitting apart*].


2


[*We leave Liverpool Street station, struggling to drag the pram full of boxes on the escalator*].
- **Are you feeling better?**
- Yes, sorry for my meltdown just now. I have not cried since those gipsies raided my vaping shop...
- **Well, to be fair you also cried two hours ago after puking your guts in Serena's house. And also, when you saw the amaretti in the deli.**
**It is all good, though. Sometimes it is good to cry, come on...**

- Speak for yourself, perhaps it is good among you bloody intellectuals. Crying sucks. It makes me feel like a failure.

- **Well, but you are not.**

- Okay, yeah, shut up now.

[*He sees Lorenzo near the exit chatting to a girl. We walk to him*].

< Hello, little rascals! It has been so long! This is Aasha, from Mumbai [*he introduces the girl to us*].

# Hi, guys! Nice to meet you.

[*We greet her back and we introduce ourselves, and then the four of us start walking towards Shoreditch*].

< So? What is new?

- Well, look… [*Gaetano does not even have the time to start the sentence, as Lorenzo interrupts him after a moment*].

< Hold on a second, you can tell me everything in a bit. First, I wanted to announce that Aasha and I are about to start our own start-up!

- **Congratulations, it is great!**

[*Gaetano does not show interest and looks impatient*].

< We met at that Brick Lane fair during the networking hour. We found out that we are quite similar, but specifically, we have the same goals. She wanted to start her own business as well, and so, here we are now.

Her father is one of the biggest businessmen in the area of private transportation in Mumbai, and she has just finished a Master's in Business Administration at Cass Business School, one of the most prestigious English universities – and of the world – in its field.

She has just met me tonight, after work, as we were planning on finishing up the last administrative bits and bobs to fill in, in order to start the company as soon as we can.

- **What is the company all about?**

< Yes! I was waiting for this question. Prepare yourselves.

We would love to start a business of double-decker buses offering brunches, lunches, and snacks during London tours. Yes, right on those buses.

This way, after seeing Trafalgar Square or the London Eye, you can also taste scrumptious pie and mash, listening to a recorded guide which explains the history of these important places. Genius, right?

We wanted to call it "The Gusti-bus".

[*He expected us to show some excitement, but instead what we felt was nothing but pure and deep embarrassment*].

So? Any thoughts?

- **It surely is something new...**

< Yes, we think the same.

Aasha's father knows so many people here in London that would be able to help, for example to purchase the first bus at a decent price. But the most interesting thing is that Cass offers to each one of their graduates – if they start a new business – to pay for a medium to long-term commercial office lease, for their new company. Not to mention all those loans! Sometimes we even reach millions of pounds invested, MILLIONS.

[*He was almost bouncing off the walls at this point*].

Considering all this, we surely can grow in no time. I am already dreaming of opening a branch in Paris, the another in Madrid and, why not, another one in Rome. Clearly, in those instances, the food will reflect the tradition of the location...

[*Suddenly, an absent-minded Gaetano hits a step with his pram, making a wheel drop. Unluckily, all of the boxes slide into a puddle*].

- MA PORCACCIA DI QUELLA... [*Gaetano abruptly interrupts Lorenzo's speech by shouting a loud blasphemy*].

# What's happening, what did he say? [*Aasha asks Lorenzo*].

< Nothing, he is just speaking French.

Right, so what is this? How did you manage to do that? What is this stuff? [*Lorenzo asks Gaetano*].

- Instead of asking questions, why aren't you helping me!? Businessman, my ass. [*Gaetano snaps back while he is trying to pick up the boxes, now partly soaked and crooked*].
# *Is he French? [Aasha asks Lorenzo again, with no response*].
< Right, calm down now… [*Lorenzo tries to ease Gaetano's tones, but he also notices the brand on those boxes*].
DOGE? What are you doing with those scammers' stuff? Have you not read what they are about? Every Facebook post in Italians in London talks about them…
- I don't care. [*He manages to put the boxes back on the pram, but at the same time Lorenzo is clearly mortified by Gaetano's attitude*].
# Mmh, I think I should go home…
- Ah, ok! Are you sure?
# Yep.
< Ok, see you later. Good night, thank you for coming!
# See ya!
[*Aasha realised that there was some serious tension between the two, and that during the walk she would not have been considered, so she leaves us. There are now just the three of us*].
- Fuck this, the pram is totally gone… [*He tries fixing the wheel, but it is so broken that any effort is wasted*].
- **Well, you know, all you have to do is move the boxes' weight toward the less damaged part of the pram, to get some balance. Like this, it should hold for a bit.**
[*The suggested fix worked, Gaetano thanks me*].
- Bloody step…
< You know something that makes me mad about English people? That when something unfortunate happens to them, they do not spend hours complaining about this and that and blaming *Tizio, Caio and Sempronio*[29], or a step. No. They just

---

[29] The Italian version for Tom, Dick and Harry.

shut up. They set their minds at rest and tell themselves, "okay, this happened", and then they carry on. Then, they rush to think about the solution to something in order to fix what is wrong – provided there is a solution – and if there is no fix, they stop caring. They do not dwell on stuff as Italians do.

I find this way of thinking and – as a result – of acting, incredible. It is so much straighter to the point, much clearer.

- Nobody complained, oh... [*Gaetano's tone becomes more high-pitched now*].

< You have just done. Italians really have this way of doing things that gets on my nerves so badly, mainly due to their mental resistance to change, which eventually turns into a practical one.

This is why I feel so sad for those people who, just like plants, stay in the exact same spot you left them in.

Living in the same place, hanging out with the same people, avoiding confrontation, and allowing things to remain the exact same. Not to mention their innate racism and homophobia. Coward people, who once arrived in London start saying horrible things – things they really believe in – convinced that just because they are abroad, they can say whatever they want without being understood by anyone.

The best thing about the Brits is that they have money, though they spend it on the wrong things. But at least stuff works here. Not like in Italy, where once at the post office or at the bank you never know where to stand because nobody can queue decently. And when you ask, "Where is the back of the queue?", nobody can really tell you where it actually is. And then, you need to insist. If you are lucky, some old man can point to some other old man, but then this last one gets upset because he is not really at the back of anything, so he points to some middle-aged woman, who in turns starts denying it and everybody starts fighting. So, what are you left to do? You

laugh, but with a heavy heart because, when all is said and done, you still do not know where the queue starts and ends.
See, Gaetano, you are just like them. And I get really annoyed when I am with you, I almost feel hatred. You are a constant waste of time. An attention-seeking toddler, who keeps asking for favours without never giving anything back. I bet you wanted to see me tonight to ask me for yet another favour.
Honestly, I do not even know why Martina is with someone like you, but surely you must be wondering that, too.
[*These last words irritate Gaetano so much that, blinded by anger, he tackles Lorenzo and pushes him to the floor. A few punches hit the beardless young guy, who takes it all without being able to even react.*
*Feeling sorry for the whole situation, I try to separate Gaetano from Lorenzo, trying to move him away*].
- I WILL DESTROY YOU. I SWEAR I WILL KILL YOU. [*Gaetano tries wiggling out of my hold, while around us, curious faces start gathering*].
< You did not do shit to me [*he spits a few drops of blood, coming from his gums*].
- I KNOW YOU ARE SHAGGING MARTINA, ADMIT IT.
< No, wait a second. What?
Never. I am asexual, Gaetano. A romantic asexual, to be precise [*he tells us while getting back up from the floor, wiping his trousers*].
[*Gaetano calms down, while the crowd leaves*].
- What's that?
< That I do not feel the need to have intercourse with anyone, let alone a relationship.
- Does this mean you are not fucking Martina?
< Yeah, I am not doing any of that. I am not shagging anyone, Gaetano, I am not interested in that.
- That means Serena was wrong…

< Of course, Serena was wrong. Why do you still believe in what that moron says?
- Shut up. Why are you asexual?
< What kind of question is that? There is no explanation, I always felt like that.
- Right.
< Cool.
- Why have you never told me this?
< Because they are not things that the world needs to know, some stuff about my life I prefer to keep private, you know.
- But I'm… was… am I still your friend?
< Yes, if you want.
- Well, I don't want to. You have just told me so much nasty stuff, even that you hate me when we hang out together…
< You know that these are nothing else but displays of affection, come on.
- Since when?
< Always.
- Ah.
[Gaetano looks at Lorenzo and Lorenzo stares back, embarrassed about what has just happened].
< Pint?
- Buckfast[30]. From the off-licence.
< I am not even sure I know what that is, but yeah.
- **You two scare me.**

3


[We leave the off-licence holding a Buckfast bottle, while Gaetano keeps pushing the pram despite the clear difficulties].
< You can't fix problems by drinking on your own. You can do that if you drink with someone else, right Gaetà?

---

[30] A brand of caffeinated fortified wine, most common amongst the young.

- Stop quoting old people and pass me this awfulness.
< Yeah, it does not look good.
- You really must try it then…
[*We sit on a bench in a nearby square to drink*].
- This city tires you out badly. It chews you and spits you out when you are nothing else but old mush.
[*Silence falls suddenly*].
You know, last night I dreamt that I was able to do the splits effortless, just like in the past… I was super disappointed when I woke up.
- **What does London have to do with your ability to do splits?**
- Nothing, Marco. I just associated in my mind a picture of myself doing a full split with another image of me being all over the place here, right now.
I think I'm rather tired of this city. I'm tired of eating bad food. When you cook a piece of chicken there's just so much water everywhere, not to mention the vegetables! If you are lucky to find any good ones, they taste nothing. I'm tired of not being able to find good pasta sauces at the supermarket, of all those plastic-tasting meal deals.
I'm tired of paying to live.
Wasting three-quarters of my salary to pay for my rent, for various household expenses and transport, spending the rest on weed and alcohol, just not to think of this daily misery.
A dog chasing its tail. This is simply not a life worth living.
I can't live in a place where I need to wash my ass in a sink because there's no such thing as a bidet, in this goddamn place.
I'm tired of the fact that I can't have a family of my own because I'm too busy surviving.
I'm tired of feeling lonely. Of the fact that I feel as if everything and everyone rejects me, or that they see me as waste, as nothing else but another immigrant, unable to live in a cold and merciless place like this, where everyone thinks for themselves

and never for the people around them. Having a career is so frivolous. Fuck off Lorenzo.

[*Lorenzo does not even try to give him an answer, he pretends not to hear him*].

I'm also tired of social media. Of this constant display of happiness when I can't think of a single fucking reason to be. I also don't trust those people who are always smiling in pictures, grinning. They're so creepy. The same goes for those who are always tanned, even in winter. Again, how can I not mention those people who only post selfies on their Instagram feed? I wish I could stroke them quietly, telling them they are bad people.

I'm so tired of the overall hypocrisy. No, come on, that's too corny. I'm sick and tired of people taking off their shoes on buses and such: this really pisses me off. It's full of those people here. And then again, those who throw up on each other. "You did the same!", you would say.

I'm tired of not getting considered by Martina, you know.

I'm not even sure if I can call her my girlfriend anymore, now that I think about the fact that she never did so with me, who knows.

I'm tired of this shit [*he kicks the pram which makes the boxes fall on the pavement*] and of awful they taste. I don't even think that what they told me about these is legit anymore.

I'm tired, guys.

< I am happy you realised all this by yourself.

**- Remember that you are also tired because it has been a full day of being out and about. Maybe you should rest...**

- No, wait a minute, I need to understand something [*he finishes the Buckfast*]. Do you think Martina ever loved me?

< Gaetano, you need to know this...

- How should I know?

< Have you ever said "*ti amo*", for example?

- I told her a billion times.

- **What about her to you?**
- Well, now that I think about it, maybe once. Through the intercom, one of the first times I went to see her at her place, in Sora.
I still remember that moment: I buzzed outside her house, she answers me with this lovely voice asking, "Who is it?" and I say, "It's me, Gaetano", and then she goes "*Ehi, ti amo*". And she opened the gate.
My heart races whenever I think about that.
< Are you sure? I feel it would make more sense if she said "*Ehi, ti apro*"[31], at least I reckon so.
- Are you sure?
< Well, yeah.
- To be fair, it does make sense.
< You see, you have yet another clue to make up your mind. If I can tell you something as a friend, with all that I know about your relationship, I think that you put Martina onto a pedestal and at the end of it all, she sees you as an acquaintance...
It is strange that you have not noticed it, though. How many girlfriends have you had in your life?
- Just her...
< Well, there you go, here is your answer.
The fact that she does not message you, or better, that she messages you when she needs something. The fact that you kiss *a ogni morte di Papa*[32]. These are really important answers, Gaetano. You should seriously consider moving on, at this point.
- But I'm nothing without her, I would feel even more alone...
< That is not true, you are not alone. Stop saying these things.
- **The other day Serena told me that she would still think that you are a good person even if you were to hit her or something.**

---

[31] Italian translation for: "Okay, come in".
[32] Italian translation for the saying meaning "Once in a blue moon". Literal translation: "Every time the Pope dies".

- I would never hit her, though.
So, do you think Martina left me already and I did not realise any of it?
< No, Gaetano... You have never been with Martina, it is different.
- Ah. Then, why did everything seem so real to me?
< Well, each one of us feels things differently.
- Do you really think that? Maybe.
Okay, then what about all the kisses?
< How many kisses are you talking about?
- Around four. No, five, in a year and a half. Not bad, eh?
< Gaetano, even if I never really experienced any of this, I could tell you that it is not normal in a relationship. You should kiss five times a day, not five in a year. I mean, this is what I see in movies.
I have known you for a while and I know Martina: at this point it is my duty to tell you that I feel as if you tried to keep this ideal of Martina, that everything else has just crumbled around you. That is why you are feeling this way.
- ...
I'm not sure I understood what you said, but thanks for the nice words.
< No worries.
- However, I would like to talk with Martina again, so that she can tell me whether she ever loved me. Just to make sure.
[*He gets up from the bench and starts walking toward the metro*].
< What are you doing now?
- Going yours, at this point.
- **What about all these boxes, the pram... are you leaving them all here?**
- Yeah, fuck fomodopamine.
< Gaetano, are you sure? You risk having your heart broken in no time.

- Yeah, let me rip the Band-Aid off once and for all!
[*We get up as well and we walk together*].
Right, there's something else though, a tiny thing. Lorenzo, can I sleep at your place tonight? Just tonight. I gave my bed to Serena because she got kicked out of her flat because of me. I'm not telling you all the details. It's just that I have nowhere to stay.
< You do not have to ask me; you need to ask Martina.
You are not sleeping in my bed.
- Okay, that's a yes then!
- **Guys, I think this is the end of it for us. I need to go back to my Airbnb as my flight leaves early tomorrow morning.**
< What, already?
- No, Marco, you are not going anywhere. You told me we would get a double room right here in London. You can't abandon me as well…
- **Gaetano, *you* said this…**
I am so happy to have met both of you. Please keep me updated…
- I'm going to miss you, Marco.
- **I will miss you too, Gaetano.**
< Marco, as soon as I am down in Tuscany, I will let you know, and we can meet up. Christmas is just in a few days…
- **I doubt you will see me there; I have been living in Milan for a few months now.**
**But yeah, let's keep in touch.**
- I knew you sounded like someone from Milan, bastard! Damn you!
< Have a safe trip!
[*We say goodbye just like this, rather hastily and almost painlessly*].

The "Report of Italians in the World" by Migrantes Foundation estimates that Italy is the fourth most common European nationality when it comes to the number of foreign homeless people living on the streets of London, after Romanian, Polish, and Lithuanian citizens.

**EPILOGUE**

In the four days I spent in London, I was able to witness the living conditions of three young Italian people.

I had to replace some regional and dialectal terms in the interviews' transcription, as the reader would have had some difficulty in understanding some words.

I decided not to cut or abridge any event or episode because it is essential to show how these people were interacting within a totally unfamiliar environment and how they were trying to live a normal and ordinary life. Some of them have managed to settle in, albeit sometimes with clear difficulties, whereas others struggle with the vibrancy of the city, and with finding the necessary tools to deal with everything.

Online magazines, newspapers and television shows keep mentioning Italian people who chose to live abroad, but everything is always about mere statistics and numbers, and not often enough do they talk about their stories and the reasons why they felt they wanted to leave Italy behind.

Contrary to popular belief, financial reasons are not the only motives making people emigrate. Each individual has their own reason to do so and, as such, we must try and reframe the media narrative of a country constantly failing to value its youth by reviewing and updating our understanding of this multifaceted issue.

Young people need to be heard and can't only be considered when the productivity of society is involved or seen at risk. Similarly, society itself must prevent young people from depending on older generations, by trying to be less distracted and more unified.


Marco Valdo, December 2017
London

# Acknowledgements and Contacts

Thanks to my parents, who showed their utmost support even for this project, especially during the hardest moments.

Thanks to Soukaina for once again having been the first to read these chapters and for having tolerated – and supported – my initial doubts.

Thanks to Tom and Bolla for suggesting this incredible title and having listened to this new-born creation's first cries.

Thanks to Chiara, for having translated everything into English in such a short amount of time.

Thanks to Maria Iside and Giovanni for their vital advice and their willingness to endure my pre-publication moods.

Thanks to Giulio and Eleonora for shedding some light on doubts about Ciociaria's regional idioms, and to Alba and Beatrice about Venetian dialect.

Thanks to Irene, Morgana, Valerio, Riccardo, Lorenzo, Barbara, Tommaso, friends who received the first drafts and gave me their opinions and food for thought, as well as suggestions for corrections. You saved me.

Thanks to my former Pergola Paddington's colleagues for pushing me to write despite those endless and tiring shifts we shared together. It was short but intense.

Thanks to all those Italians in London I met because they are a community of their own, unique in their own special way, who have inspired this book. You are unbelievable, I admire you all very much.

If you like the book, if you want to write a review or simply tell everyone it sucked, please write your feedback on either Amazon or Goodreads!

If you are an Italian in London and you feel that I have described you as yet another stereotype, feel free to reach out!

You will find me here:

| | |
|---|---|
| **E-mail** | Filippo_Pasqui@live.it |
| **Twitter** | @flpsq |
| **Instagram** | @nedox |
| **Telegram** | @flpsq |
| **Facebook** | Filippo Pasqui |

Should you wish to read some other work of mine, you are more than welcome to have a look at another book I wrote: "*Racconti di BlaBlaCar – Piccole storie assurde di autostop organizzati*", which is on Amazon but is only available in italian for the time being.

You can find *L'Ondhon* in italian. Search the original title "*L'Ondra*" on Amazon.

INDEX

First paperback edition, February 2021